Dear Reader,

I'm a Court TV and crime-drama junkie. I also learned from my family that laughter is an essential ingredient in life. Call me weird, you won't be the first. But I have this horrible problem with wanting to inject humor into everything. In fact, when I first began submitting work to publishers, they kept telling me that I made them laugh in inappropriate places.

Trust me, I took the hint, and decided murder and laughter didn't mix. Then I got feisty. There had to be a happy medium. Thus, *Without a Clue* was born, where I could have a murder mystery that's gone horribly wrong. Or wonderfully right, if you're a lover of lovers.

So this book is a nod to all of the things that float my boat. Love, laughter, murder, mayhem and a mystery with no possible solution except to decide everyone's guilty of *something*.

I wish you all plenty of love, plenty of mayhem, plenty of reading and plenty of fun!

Trish Jensen

"What now?" Matt asked, his voice a little gravelly as he turned from the open doorway in the bedroom

"We...uh, explore the secret passageway?"

He sort of liked that Meg put it in the form of a question. It left open other possibilities.

Matt checked his watch. "Probably not enough time right now. We have to get me ready to be murdered."

Her eyes took on a wicked light. "Now the good times are starting to roll."

"A guy could develop a complex," he said, but he let her go.

She showed him how to close the secret passageway again, and they returned to the bedroom suite.

"Let's check the weapon," Meg said, reaching for the stage knife.

"Bloodthirsty little wench, aren't you?"

She smiled. "You betcha."

WITHOUT A CLUE

Trish Jensen

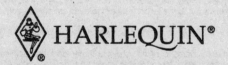

HARLEQUIN®

TORONTO • NEW YORK • LONDON
AMSTERDAM • PARIS • SYDNEY • HAMBURG
STOCKHOLM • ATHENS • TOKYO • MILAN • MADRID
PRAGUE • WARSAW • BUDAPEST • AUCKLAND

ISBN 0-373-44208-4

WITHOUT A CLUE

Copyright © 2005 by Patricia G. Jensen.

All rights reserved. Except for use in any review, the reproduction or utilization of this work in whole or in part in any form by any electronic, mechanical or other means, now known or hereafter invented, including xerography, photocopying and recording, or in any information storage or retrieval system, is forbidden without the written permission of the publisher, Harlequin Enterprises Limited, 225 Duncan Mill Road, Don Mills, Ontario, Canada M3B 3K9.

All characters in this book have no existence outside the imagination of the author and have no relation whatsoever to anyone bearing the same name or names. They are not even distantly inspired by any individual known or unknown to the author, and all incidents are pure invention.

This edition published by arrangement with Harlequin Books S.A.

® and TM are trademarks of the publisher. Trademarks indicated with ® are registered in the United States Patent and Trademark Office, the Canadian Trade Marks Office and in other countries.

www.eHarlequin.com

Printed in U.S.A.

ABOUT THE AUTHOR

Trish Jensen once wanted to be famous. But she decided to be a writer instead.

Life is still sweet. She lives in the gorgeous mountains of central Pennsylvania with the love of her life, Ross, and the banes of her existence, dog Cassie and cat Foxy.

E-mail is welcome at trishjensen@earthlink.net. Or you are welcome to yell at her editor at the Harlequin address. Send snail mail c/o MTH, 233 Broadway, Suite 1001, New York, NY 10279.

Books by Trish Jensen

HARLEQUIN LOVE & LAUGHTER
24—THE HARDER THEY FALL

This book is dedicated with much love to a bunch of loopy women who help me wake up with a smile every single day. Humor is such a powerful thing. Thank you, ladies (you, *of course*, know who you are) for empowering me constantly.

1

"OUR CORPSE IS DRUNK."

Megan Renshaw glanced up from the script before her. Her assistant, Tina Brown, stood at the entrance to the study of the old Charleston plantation. "Pardon me?"

Tina stomped farther into the room, hands planted on slim hips. "You heard me. Our corpse has arrived. And he's high as a kite."

Megan sat back and dropped her pen. "Well, he has time to sober up. The paying guests don't arrive until Friday."

"A cement truck could land on that man's head and he wouldn't feel it."

"This isn't a problem," Megan said, sliding back her chair and standing. "We'll get Glenda to pour some coffee down him."

Tina scowled. "Drunk and drunker."

Megan checked her watch. "Already? It's not even three."

"She's been using the 'two for you and one for

me' method while experimenting with the Marsala sauce for tomorrow night's veal."

Megan winced. "Do we need to buy more Marsala?"

Tina's frown deepened. "Only if she adds it to the eggs again tomorrow morning."

Megan laughed as she headed to the door. "So that's what that flavor was this morning."

Tina followed, hot on her heels. "Remind me again why we keep her?"

"You mean other than the fact that she makes a crème brûlée to die for?"

"Only after she's cracked open the brandy." They headed down the hall to the front foyer of the mansion. "It also doesn't hurt she's the boss's cousin," Tina said under her breath.

Grinning, Megan replied, "Doesn't hurt a bit."

Tina scowled at her. "This weekend hasn't even begun and already we've got half the staff blitzed. I smell disaster."

Tina always smelled disaster. "Not exactly half the staff. We're still waiting on our butler, our chambermaid and four of our 'invited guests.' I'm certain at least one of them will be sober."

"You're inhumanly unflappable, Meg," Tina grumbled. "Does anything ever faze you?"

Megan refrained from mentioning that she hadn't taken being left at the altar all that well four years ago. Of course, by the next day she'd decided Mike had done her a huge favor. And right now she was frankly ecstatic. If she'd married Mike, she'd probably be a stay-at-home mother by now, instead of special events coordinator for Big Adventures Travel.

And she loved her job. Adored it. True, crises like this one arose on a regular basis, but that's what kept the job interesting. And challenging.

This weekend was the most important event to date, career-wise, though. It was the launch of Big Adventures's murder mystery theme package. It was also her baby. She'd presented the idea to her boss, Roy Lucas, a year ago. He'd been skeptical that she'd be able to find enough people who met the requirements necessary to make the venture profitable. By her count, the clients only needed two. A love of a good whodunit and nice, fat wallets.

"The guy isn't going to be in any shape to walk through dress rehearsal tonight," Tina muttered.

"What's to rehearse? He gives one speech at the beginning of supper, then disappears until he's found dead."

They entered the large marbled foyer, and Meg immediately spotted their corpse slouching on a receiving couch, blowing at the fronds of a potted palm. By the slackness of his jaw and the glaze in his brown eyes, she realized Tina hadn't been exaggerating. The man was sloshed. Meg would have to call the agency next week and request sober actors from here on out. She didn't think that was asking too much.

She sifted through her brain trying to come up with the man's name. He'd been hired to play Lionel De Wynter, the supposed owner of this mansion, and the host for the supper where the mystery began.

That's right, Terence Brogan. Formerly a Shakespearean actor, lately reduced to bit TV parts and commercials. Even stoned, he exuded an imperious air that would work well in his role as the evil corporate raider, about to announce to his "guests" his nefarious scheme.

His hair was graying gracefully, and his eyebrows held a sinister bent. His Roman nose gave him the natural look of a snob. Perfect. Just as soon as he stopped drooling.

"Mr. Brogan?" Meg said, stopping before him and thrusting out her hand. "I'm Megan Renshaw."

Although the two had talked on the phone several times—most of which were spent with him dissecting his motivation for playing a dead guy— this was Terence Brogan's first job for Big Adventures. Possibly his last if he always had this much trouble struggling to his feet and focusing. Instead of shaking her outstretched hand, he grasped it, turned it palm down and almost plowed into her as he began to bend down, thought better of it, and instead lifted it to his lips to press a gallantly drunken—and thankfully not slobbery—kiss upon her skin.

When he finally managed to connect after a couple of aborted attempts, his foggy eyes swept over her and his palm went to his breastbone. "'She walksh in be-beauty, like the night,'" he intoned, "'as if all the world were his stage. Of cloudlesh climes and st-starry nights; And all that's best of dark and night...'" He stopped, looking momentarily confused. "Wait, wait, that should be 'bright. All that's best of dark and bright.'"

Much as she enjoyed a good Byron poem, Meg didn't have all day. "That's lovely. Truly. What a very dear man you are. And that delivery! Why, I knew straight off, just from your photo and impressive résumé, that you were quite a catch." She waved in Tina's direction. "And this is my assistant, Tina Brown."

"A pleasure, madam," the actor said, without moving his head an iota in Tina's direction.

"Tina, why don't you take Mr. Brogan to the kitchen and offer him some of Glenda's wonderful coffee, while Timmy takes Mr. Brogan's suitcase—" that's when she noticed the steamer trunk, the large suitcase and the industrial size makeup case flanking the man "—er, while Timmy and I take his luggage to his room."

Thank goodness the mansion sported an elevator that ran to all three floors.

Brogan's eyes widened a moment, and once again his palm dramatically covered his heart. "Why, madam, are you under the mish-mistaken impression that I am inebriated?"

Tina snorted.

"You're not?" Meg said dubiously. If this was sober, they were in even bigger trouble.

"Sh-certainly not! I'm a professional, I'll have you know."

"Of course you are," she rushed to assure him. "A recent blow to the head, perhaps?"

He looked mildly offended, but shook his head and his hand came up to cover his jaw. "Emergency root canal shurgery."

Meg blew out a relieved breath. "Oh, I'm so sorry to hear that. The Novocain hasn't worn off, I take it."

"I had the shurgery Monday. However, it'sh still quite painful."

Terrific. Pain pills. If she couldn't talk the man into putting them away for the rest of the weekend, she might have to sneak into his room and steal them. It wouldn't do for the first corpse of her first murder mystery weekend not to be able to say his lines clearly, although she had the feeling he'd make a believable stiff.

That was her last thought just before Terence

Brogan's eyes rolled to the back of his head, and he pitched forward, straight into her arms.

MATT ROSSI WAS RIDING OUT the biggest endorphin rush in his entire thirty-six-year life. Catching the touchdown pass that won his high school the state championship his senior year had nothing on this. Getting inside Nina Chambers's panties in eleventh grade had nothing on this. Hell, making his first million dollars at the age of thirty-two had had nothing on this.

As he drummed his thumbs on the steering wheel of his vintage blue Mustang convertible, in beat with the music of Harry Connick, Jr. blaring from his speakers, Matt decided he was definitely the master of his fate. The keeper of his destiny. The maker of his dreams.

Yesterday he'd signed a land development deal so huge and so profitable he could never work another day in his life and he'd still have money to spare when he died at a hundred. Even with the bunch of kids he planned on having. Even with lavishing his wife with expensive gifts every day of their marriage.

His bubble burst just a tad at that. In truth, he didn't have a wife yet. Or any kids that he knew about for that matter. But now that this deal had been successfully completed, it was time to move on down his checklist.

Graduate high school. Check.

Earn a college scholarship. Check.

Graduate college. Check.

Work hard for several years and save and scrape. Check.

Open own real estate development company. Check.

Make a fortune. Check.

Start a family. No go.

Not yet, anyway, although in truth he'd been awfully busy checking off all those other items to really begin an honest search for Ms. Right. He'd kept his eyes peeled over the years, just in case she popped into his life at any given moment. But so far, it was still a no go. He'd correct that now. He was taking time off from work to search in that systematic way he approached every challenge he tackled.

And really, his standards weren't out in left field, either. All he was asking for was an intelligent, funny, beautiful, sexy, orderly woman who was interested in settling down and making babies. Lots and lots of babies.

He wanted a houseful of them. He'd grown up the only son of "Brick" and Maria Rossi, both of whom had worked tirelessly; his father as a bricklayer and his mother a cleaning lady. Consequently he'd been left alone much of the time. Too much of the time. What he wouldn't have given for younger brothers and sisters to fill the void, to be companions. And his personal slaves.

No kid of his was going to grow up an only child. Therefore his wife would have to agree to a houseful of them. Of course, he also enjoyed peace and solitude, so she'd have to be good at keeping them quiet, too. Noise and chaos drove him crazy.

As he reached the outskirts of Charleston, he conjured a vision of a wife and kids filling the Charleston mansion he'd invested in at an auction three years ago. He'd originally checked it out as merely another good investment. But the first time he'd laid eyes on the Southern Georgian, he knew it was perfect for his future family. The mansion was huge, with seventeen bedrooms and two guest cottages out back. He could produce a whole passel of children without having everyone tripping over one another. It'd be big and peaceful and orderly.

Smiling, he made the left onto Magnolia Lane, the mile-long drive that led to his, only his home. No pesky neighbors to contend with. Another plus.

Whistling, he enjoyed the secluded solitude the huge live oaks dripping with Spanish moss afforded him. Yes, indeed, he'd chosen well. He certainly hoped the Realtor maintaining the place had made certain the cleaning service was doing their job. He wasn't into dust.

His whistling stopped in mid-toot when he emerged from the tunnel of foliage and passed through the brick gates, and into the mansion's cul de sac. There had to be ten cars parked in his driveway! What the hell?

Pulling in to the first available spot, he cut the engine and practically leapt from the car. A scowl tugged at his lips as he passed car after trespassing car. It grew even fiercer when he looked up the steps between the giant columns to find the oak double doors thrown wide open.

Racing up the stairs two at a time, all kinds of thoughts were scrambling through his head. Especially the one of how he was about to murder a Realtor.

He reached the door and stopped dead in his tracks. The sight that greeted him nearly made his eyes bug out.

Chaos reigned.

2

Meg waved as best she could at their new arrival. He looked a little dumbfounded, which was probably natural, considering she was using an unconscious man's hand to deliver the greeting. But her corpse was her only tool at the moment. The rest of his sprawled self had the rest of her sprawled self plastered to the marble floor.

"I'll be right with you," she kind of grunted, as she heaved with all her might until Mr. Brogan rolled off her body and ended up spread-eagled on his back.

Now another dilemma presented itself. How to gracefully rise from the floor in a skirt that wasn't constructed to give much leeway unless she hiked it up around her thighs. So thinking quickly, she rolled onto her stomach pushed to her knees, then one leg at a time got to her feet.

She ran a hand through her hair before turning around to face the newest guest. For some reason his lips were slightly parted and he was staring at her midsection. She had the feeling he'd just taken in an eyeful of her butt poked high in the air.

She jumped over Terence, her hand outstretched. "Hi, I'm Megan. Are you the butler?"

"Excuse me?"

"One of the paid guests?"

"Excuse me?!"

Meg dropped her hand, seeing as he looked too dumbfounded to shake it. He was really cute, but apparently a little dim. "Are you lost?" she suggested. That was a better option than an escapee from a mental institution. Last time she checked, they didn't have any straitjackets on hand.

His brown eyes cleared a little and he shook his head. "No, but you must be. I'm Matt Rossi and this is my property."

Meg took a step back, took a deep breath, then plastered a smile on her face. "Thank you so much for renting it to us."

"I didn't rent it to you."

"Well, um, yes, you did."

"I think I would know, don't you?"

Okay, he wasn't all that cute. Well, he was, but in a downer sort of way. "We signed a contract."

"Who are *we?* I know I didn't sign anything."

Terence Brogan began to moan pitifully, and Meg glanced around to see all the witnesses frozen like statues, including Tina. This wasn't good. "How about we go to my office and talk about this?"

Both of his brows lifted. *"Your* office?"

Nope, he wasn't in the least bit cute. His hair was too black and his jaw was too square and his nose was crooked. Meg conceded that his mouth was sexy, but what came out of it wasn't. "Yes, my office. At least for the duration of our…of the lease."

"Well, then, by all means, let's go to *your* office."

MATT WAS FLOORED. It had been like walking into a Laurel and Hardy movie that was freeze-framed. Everybody who'd been in motion had gone still, and the one still person had arisen from the debris of the wreckage and taken charge.

He needed to regroup fast. Except, the woman who had risen from the carnage had a smile that could scramble eggs. And his eggs needed to stay intact. As far as he could tell, his home had been invaded without his consent. And apparently this brain scrambler was claiming they had legal permission to invade. If she was right, there was going to be one hurtin' Realtor in Charleston.

"Follow me," the woman said, as if he needed a guide.

Gladly, he decided after catching the view.

She led him down the maze of hallways to the study. *His* study. Which she had confiscated and turned into *her* office.

He seemed to vaguely take in that she was chatting pleasantly the entire time. But scrambling did strange things to his brain because all he was digesting were words like "murder" and "guests." He wasn't into murder as a rule and he most definitely wasn't into guests. *Any* guests.

They reached the study and she took command of the desk as if she owned it, smiling while she offered him the guest chair.

If she hadn't used the smile, he might have tossed her straight out the bay window. But her mouth and face were weapons he had a hard time overcoming.

She had rust-brown hair that fell in wisps to her jaw, and gray eyes that defied description. She smelled good. And that butt moved right. He'd never known there were wrongs and rights in butt-moving before, but he knew right when he saw it swaying in front of him.

Nonetheless, she was an intruder, and therefore had to be considered the enemy.

"Mr…?"

"Rossi. Matt Rossi. And this is my house, Ms…?"

"Renshaw. But call me Meg. And we're thrilled to be able to use this spectacular house for our mystery weekend."

"Don't be so thrilled. You have no right to be here."

"As I said, we've signed a lease," she said, rooting through a file drawer.

"That my agent had no right to draw up."

She pulled it out, still serene as all get-out. "He told us he has the authority to sign off on anything to do with the maintenance of this house."

She was right, but he wasn't willing to concede that easily. "Renting it to intruders technically is *not* maintenance."

"We're *not* intruders. We paid for the privilege to use it."

That fact finally hit him. "Is this your first time here?"

"Yes, it is," she said, smiling even brighter. "And it's perfect."

Matt took the lease from her hands and perused it. "You know, I could have you evicted," he said, between clenched teeth.

She nodded. "You go right ahead and begin eviction proceedings first thing in the morning. By my calculations we'll have been gone at least three weeks by the time they come to toss our butts out."

Right again. As long as they'd signed the lease in good faith, it would probably take weeks before he could legally have them kicked to the curb. This wasn't good. "Okay, the lease says that you pay for cleanup and any and all damages that might occur during your occupancy."

Her mouth popped open and she waved at the papers. "You barely glanced at that thing. How do you know that?"

Matt shrugged. "I read fast."

"Wow, that's pretty impressive."

He'd question her sincerity, but her smile actually did look genuinely impressed. And he knew she knew her rights, so she wasn't trying to butter him up. Still, he felt a twinge of pride. "Here's the deal, I'm not leaving. I'm staying to protect my investment."

Ms. Renshaw nodded. "You'll have a great time. And it only costs—"

"Don't even try it."

"—not a dime for you! Have fun on us."

"And I, of course, will be staying in the master bedroom," he added, trying to grab back *some* control over this untenable situation.

She pursed her lips and her brow furrowed. "I'm afraid that's not possible. The murder victim is going to be the owner of the mansion. It wouldn't do to have him found in a guest room."

"Kill him off in the kitchen."

She shook her head, and the light from the bay window showcased every single nuance of highlight in her hair. "Owners of mansions don't generally even know where the kitchen is."

He was about to argue until he realized that even he wasn't exactly sure where the kitchen was. "Off the dining room?" he ventured to guess.

"Do you even know where the dining room is, Mr. Rossi?" she asked, sweet as cream pudding.

"Right off the kitchen," he answered her, getting a little irritated she was grilling him. More irritated he didn't know the answers. After all, this was a *big* house. "How about killing him off in the dining room?"

She shook her head. "The script calls for him being found dead in his bed. In the *master bedroom* bed."

"Meg," a woman said, striding into the study, a look of complete consternation on her face. "We have a problem."

Matt recognized her from the foyer. She was tall and skinny with a face that might be pretty if she smiled once in a while. Great, he had a smiler and a frowner on his hands. Both female. It almost felt as if he was caught in a cosmic estrogen tornado.

"Tina, this is Mr. Rossi, owner of this property," Ms. Renshaw said. "Mr. Rossi, Tina Brown."

"Hiya," Ms. Brown said, with a perfunctory smile, which vanished instantly. "Meg, Mr. Brogan isn't going to be delivering any speeches anytime soon. He's really whacked out on those drugs."

"You have drugs in my house?" Matt said.

"Prescription," the Renshaw woman said quickly. She tapped her jaw. "Root canal." She looked from him to Tina. "We'll have to improvise. Maybe he can play the silent but sinister butler. This isn't a problem."

"Meg, we need a corpse. One that can read his lines."

Matt couldn't figure out how a corpse would need lines, and he wasn't sure he wanted to know.

Megan Renshaw began tapping her lips with one finger. Then her head swiveled in his direction. "Are you as quick at memorizing as you are at reading?"

Uh-oh. "Well, technically, I guess. But—"

"And you want to sleep in your own bed in the master suite, right?"

"Since I own the place, I think I have the—"

She thrust out her hand. "Hello, Mr. De Wynter."

"We're dead," Tina Brown muttered.

"No, but *he* will be. Eventually."

Matt stared at the woman who was turning the most dazzling smile he'd ever seen on him. "I hope you mean that figuratively."

She grabbed his hand and pumped it. "You're hired."

3

MATT HAD LANDED in the Twilight Zone. He'd come to his house with all intentions of enjoying the serenity it had to offer, only to be greeted with Bizarro World. Worse, he was now apparently employed by a woman who by all rights should be locked in a padded cell.

Or maybe he should be for even considering the idea. But for some reason letting this woman down held no appeal. And heck, he was on vacation, and his favorite reading had always been mysteries. It might not be so bad. Maybe even fun, though even *playing* dead was a little disconcerting.

The hand she stuck out to him was soft as a flower petal against his much more callous one. And was completely swallowed by it. Although she was fairly tall for a woman, she was slender and apparently small-boned. It gave him a sense of her vulnerability.

And she was on his property. It seemed to him it was his duty to make certain he'd be there to

watch out for her. Because by the looks of everything so far, she wasn't exactly organized.

Reluctantly he dropped her hand. "How soon
after the guests arrive do I die?" he asked.

"The first night."

"And then what?"

"And then we cart you off on a gurney, and
you don't return until the mystery's been solved."

Matt shook his head. "Unacceptable. I want to
be free to keep an eye on the house and grounds
during the entire time."

Out of the corner of his eye he saw the Tina
woman roll her eyes and throw up her hands. "I'm
telling you, Meg, we're in deep trouble."

"Nonsense," Meg said. "Just give me a minute
to think."

She strolled back to the desk and sat down, and
he could practically see her wheels chugging along.

"Meg's thinking?" Tina asked. "I'm out of
here." She practically sprinted from the room.

Suddenly Meg glanced up at him and said,
"Okay, I have two possibilities. Tell me what you
think of these."

Oh, he couldn't wait.

"One, we already have a chief inspector, so
that's out. But we could add you as his assistant.
Of course, you'd have to be heavily disguised."

Matt didn't like that option for two reasons.
He'd been in charge of his own company for so

long that the thought of playing second fiddle and actually having to take orders really rankled. And second, although he wouldn't object to wearing certain clothing to play a part, disguises conjured images of fake mustaches and Coke-bottle glasses. "What's the other option?"

"You can come back as yourself."

His brows drew together. "Wouldn't that kind of ruin the mystery of who killed me?"

"Not if you come back as your spirit."

"Spirit? You mean…a ghost?"

She beamed at him as if he were five and had just conquered the concept of the alphabet. "Exactly."

"You're kidding, right?"

"Not at all."

"I don't believe in all that ghost or spirit nonsense."

Her brows lifted and he once again noticed what a beautiful shade of gray her eyes were. And how huge, especially when she was looking at him as though he was an idiot. "You *do* realize the history of this mansion, don't you?"

Matt bristled. "I bought the property, didn't I?"

"Then you know it's purported to be haunted."

No, somehow he hadn't heard that. "Bull."

She nodded. "It's the lore, and there have been documented cases from previous owners."

"It's an old house, they were just hearing the creaks and groans."

She shrugged. "I'm sure that's part of it. But a lot stranger stuff has happened around here."

"Probably made up," he interjected.

She went on as if he hadn't spoken. "The story is that in the late 1800s, the house was bought by an ex-Confederate soldier named Jamie Foster, and it had been badly damaged in the war. He refurbished it, then brought his wife from Savannah to live here. Apparently Jamie was suffering from what today we'd call post-traumatic stress disorder, and became more and more irrational and abusive toward his wife. When he subjected her to a fairly bad beating while she was pregnant, she decided she wasn't going to allow him to have any part in the raising of her child."

She paused until Matt finally said, "And?"

"She poisoned his black-eyed peas."

"Ouch."

"So legend has it that he refused to leave the home he'd built, and still haunts it to this day."

"Not that I believe any of this bull, but even if there's a hint of truth, why would anyone pay to come here?"

"Are you kidding? We played up the haunted mansion part when advertising the weekend. It's why we filled up so fast."

Matt made an involuntary grunting sound. "Some people are so gullible."

"I prefer to call them adventurous. With open minds."

He had the feeling there was an implied insult in there, even though not a hint of it showed in her serene expression. "I don't know. Playing a ghost? Would I have to wear a white sheet or anything?"

Meg laughed, a tinkling sound that was as soothing as soft music. If one liked soft music.

"Then what?"

She held up her hands as if framing him out behind a camera. "I see you in the same smoking jacket and silk pajama bottoms you're found dead in. But the clothes would be much more tattered and still blood-spattered."

"What about makeup?" he asked suspiciously.

"If anything, we'll just make your face and hands a lot more pale. And the way we'd set it up is you'll always show up in a dimly lit room, so you'll look not from this world."

"I don't know," he said, forcing skepticism into his voice he wasn't exactly feeling. Oddly enough, it sounded like a challenge, and Matt thrived on challenge.

"Do you have anything better?" she asked, eyebrows raised.

"Yes. You all relocate."

"Not an option. Try again."

Matt felt the same exhilaration he usually received haggling over a real estate deal, and it was befuddling—and different. After all, this was puff-ball stuff. And instead of wanting to break down his adversary, he sort of wanted to see her rise to the occasion. Not to win, of course. Losing wasn't an option for him. But to give him some fun in the process.

Then again, he'd already lost one battle to her. But that wasn't technically his mistake. His mistake was trusting the man he'd hired to oversee this property. That _would_ be rectified shortly.

"How about if you cast me in another part that puts me in the middle of things the entire weekend, instead of the dead guy?"

He could swear her shoulders drooped just a little, and his heart kind of pinched.

"I could do that," she said. "But all of the other roles have been cast."

"So, recast."

"I can't ask them to learn a new role on this short notice. It's just not fair. And I'm not sure of the rules, but they might charge me extra for it. Besides, that means you relinquish your bedroom."

This woman might be a little crafty, but he still figured she didn't have a clue what she was doing. "You don't have a clue what you're doing, do you?"

The shoulders straightened and stiffened, which kind of made him want to cheer.

"Listen, things were going just fine until you came along."

"Right, your dead guy was basically DOA."

"I could have found a way around that without you. You just seemed…convenient, in a really inconvenient kind of way. I'm trying to accommodate your desires while still pulling off this gig. And you're really beginning to tick me off." She paused for a breath, but before he could retort she chimed in some more. "I have the lease. As far as I can tell, *you* are the one trespassing. You could be a drifter or a squatter or something for all I know. So you can choose one of the options I've given you, or you can come up with one of your own which *I'll* approve, or you can stick it and just leave. Work with me or you're dead weight."

Whoa! Smiling and grinning and beaming and cajoling, she was beautiful. Pissed off she was absolutely stunning. Her eyes turned a dark, firecracker silver, her cheeks turned into flaming spots. Even her hair seemed to get mad at him, tossing and shimmering like molten lava.

Deadly if messed with.

But still funny. "A hobo who drove up in a Mustang?"

"Could have been stolen."

"In these clothes?"

"Stolen."

He was suddenly in the position of having to prove himself, which felt a little ludicrous. How had she turned the tables on him? "Want to see my driver's license?"

"Could have been forged."

"Talk to my lawyer?"

"Could be your bookie."

"Audit my taxes?"

"You mean you've actually filed?"

Okay, now cheeky had morphed into insulting. He was trying to prove himself to a squatter who in the last half hour had claimed she had the right to invade his home and evict him at the same time. This was reaching critical mass on his acceptable meter. She might be pretty, but she was taking the upper hand without him ever having figured out how, and that was unacceptable. But he wasn't quite sure what the next step would be. He'd encountered crooks and shady dealers and wretched lawyers, but he'd never had to deal with an adversary who demanded with such conviction that *she* was within her rights while *he* was a possible fraud.

He squelched all of the possible courses of action he could take to ruin her uppity attitude *and* her weekend, swallowed his pride and said, "I'll play the ghost."

Her anger seemed to melt from her eyes. She smiled. "Thank you," she said softly. "And I'm sorry. I really almost *never* have a temper."

Somehow he doubted that.

Once again she thrust out her hand. "I promise, you'll receive industry wages."

He almost choked. But he kept a straight face and said, "I should hope so. I don't work for free. And since I'm pulling double duty..."

"You'll get the same wage as everyone else. Scale. And be glad for it, seeing as I didn't ask to hire you. Don't push it."

He wanted to grin so badly. "Well, technically you did hire me."

"That was a choice of getting rid of you or putting your carcass to use."

"Yes, ma'am," he said. "My carcass is at your disposal."

"Don't I wish," she muttered, but then grinned. "Just teasing of course."

He wasn't so sure. Didn't Ted Bundy have an engaging smile?

"All right," she said, her voice going all practical again, "I'm going to have to do some rewrites tonight, before I can get you your script. How about if I have it delivered to your room by nine? That should give you time to memorize by—"

"Nine-fifteen."

"Sure. Yes, well, let's hope so."

"I have a better idea," Matt said, from out of nowhere that he could figure out. "How about if we meet for supper and go over the script together? I'd love to help shape my ghost character."

Meg also looked gorgeous flustered. He wondered if she'd ever be able to play a corpse because she'd probably look too good then, too. No one would ever believe it.

"I don't think—"

"I want a say in my ghost," he said.

She stared at him for a moment, then nodded. "Okay, a dinner *meeting*. In here?"

"Let's do it from the suite adjoined to my bedroom. I'd like to work out logistics."

She stared at him, narrow-eyed.

Holding up his hands, Matt assured her. "Ms. Renshaw, I have no designs on you. But whatever I do, I want it to be done right. And if I'm dying up there and clues will be planted up there, I want to talk them through." When she still continued to look skeptical, he said, "You're welcome to bring a bodyguard. How about Tina?"

Meg stared at him and laughed. "It's a deal, Mr.…"

"De Wynter. Just call me Lionel De Wynter."

VIOLIN STRINGS had nothing on Meg's nerves. Her career depended on the success of this weekend, and so far everything was shaping up about as well as her wedding day to Mike.

A disaster in the making is what it was. Her dead guy was gone, and in his place she had an overbearing, angry homeowner who was trying to call his own shots on *her* project.

So she'd spent all day feverishly rewriting much of the script to incorporate the fact that the man didn't look all that sinister. Sinfully sexy, maybe, but turning him into the twenty-first century Genghis Khan wasn't going to be easy, given he wanted to play the part sans makeup.

And it was hard to conceive of anyone wanting to rid the world of this particular male specimen. Climb into bed with him, maybe. But shoot him in bed? No.

He wanted to talk over the script. He'd had to cancel the supper meeting—which gave her a vague sense of disappointment—because an important business call had come through. So she'd had to write one herself, fast. And she wasn't a writer, she was a party planner for a travel agency.

Was it only six hours ago she'd loved her job? Right now she'd happily flip flapjacks at the local diner. At least *those* people would appreciate her efforts.

She blew a strand of hair off of her forehead, just as there was a knock on her door. "It's open," she said, with not much conviction.

Tina walked in. Just who she wanted to see. The voice of doom and gloom.

"We have a problem."

"This is news? What now?"

"Lionel De Wynter's personal assistant has just run off with the pool boy."

"They're *supposed* to run off together. It's in the script. Maybe they're rehearsing?"

"If they are, they're really into their roles. They just called from Las Vegas."

"Oh, boy."

"Let's do the same thing. Blow this pop stand and head to Vegas."

Meg tsked. "You have no imagination. We can get through this."

"Tell me how."

Meg looked at Tina speculatively. "Feel like playing the part of a personal assistant?"

Tina's hands raised defensively, and she began backing up slowly toward the door. "Not a chance, boss. I'm the behind-the-scenes person, remember?"

Sighing, Meg closed her eyes and rubbed her temples. There had to be a solution. One just wasn't popping into her head at this very moment.

Tina squeaked, and Meg glanced up sharply. Apparently an obstacle at the threshold to the office had blocked Tina's escape.

That obstacle had gorgeous brown eyes and dark hair and a mouth that screamed "kiss me." Especially when he had that lazy smile tugging at his lips.

"Excuse me," Tina managed, then ducked

under Mr. Rossi's arm and skedaddled. That was kind of a strange, skittish reaction from fairly bold and stoic Tina. And it kind of irritated Meg that this man could intimidate her assistant like no one—not even Meg—could.

Rossi glanced to his left, watching Tina make good her escape, then turned back to Meg. With a barely concealed smirk, he strolled toward the desk. Raising his eyebrows at all of the pages littering the desktop, he drawled, "Problems?"

"Nothing we can't handle," she said, trying to keep a defensive, hysterical tone from her voice.

"I hear my personal assistant jumped ship."

"Are you always into eavesdropping, Mr. Rossi?"

"Only when I happen to be standing at an open door, trying to get your attention."

Meg sighed. "Yes, we lost a couple more to the whims of passion." She snorted. "Never have seen the merit in that, but what can you do?"

"I know what *you* can do."

Meg's heart tripped a little, because the instantaneous list of things she'd like to do were a little scandalous. And shocking to even herself.

She swallowed and tried for bland. "Really? What would that be?" She picked up her water glass and sipped.

"Why don't *you* play my personal assistant?"

Water splooshed all over her desk, and she choked.

The man moved quickly around the desk and began thumping her back. "You all right?"

Meg grabbed tissues from a box and wiped her watering eyes, then mouth, then the surface of the desk. "Sure. Fine. Really."

He stopped thumping her, but began stroking her back in what should have been a soothing manner, but was failing miserably at soothing her.

His huge hands were warm and gentle and whispered seduction, even in such an innocent act.

Meg didn't even like this guy. Even though he'd agreed to step in and help out when he didn't even want them here, he was just an additional monkey wrench in what was turning out to be a disastrous venture. He wasn't the enemy—Meg didn't believe in having enemies—but he wasn't a friend, either.

So why was his touch so electrifying?

Meg wasn't into being electrocuted, either.

Finally she stood to get away from the current. "You're joking, right?"

"Why not? You have to be around all the time to oversee things anyway. If you're not part of the action, you're merely a distraction. Do it."

"Mr. Rossi—"

"My name is Matt. Call me Mr. Rossi one more time, and I'm tossing all of your butts out of here."

She'd be mad, but she couldn't quite get there when he was smiling. "Fine. Call me Ms. Renshaw one more time and I'll personally rewrite this so that it's your personal secretary who gets to kill you off."

"Does that mean you'll do it…Meg?"

She chewed on her lower lip. "Fine. Actually, it *does* make some sort of sense."

His smile grew wider, and his eyes sparkled. "Great. This should be fun."

Meg clamped her jaw shut to keep it from dropping. He actually sounded like he meant it. "I sure hope so," she finally managed.

He leaned toward her, and she had to drop her head back. That's when she noticed just how tall he really was. She was not a short woman.

"So tell me, *Meg*, am I sleeping with my personal assistant?"

4

"SINCE WHEN is the personal assistant sleeping with De Wynter?" Tina asked Meg, reading through the player profiles.

Meg never blushed. She prided herself on that. So she was certain the heat in her cheeks was simply from the heat in the room.

"You're blushing, Meg."

"I, umm, just thought I'd add a twist to the, umm, dynamics."

"Right."

Until this moment, Meg had been happily deluding herself into believing that she'd added that element just to throw off Mr. Matthew Rossi. He'd been irritating her all last evening with lists, acting like he was organizing this event instead of she.

But if she were to be brutally honest, a niggling of a fantasy had crept in to her obviously—yet heretofore unrealized—warped mind. The thought of having an affair with the man was...

Ridiculous. This wasn't like her at all. One time

she'd read a study that most men sized up women within seconds of meeting them and classified them as "yes" or "no" in the sexual sense. She'd snorted at the time. Men. It figured. She knew it had taken one look at *Christie* to make Mike decide a walk down the aisle with Meg wasn't in the plan. Well, no matter. Good riddance to Mike.

She couldn't exactly feel that way about Christie, though, considering Christie was Meg's sister. And Meg was long used to Christie stealing Meg's boyfriends. It just would have helped if Christie hadn't decided to do the stealing a day before Meg's wedding.

Then again, after the wedding would have been worse. So Mike and Christie had done her a favor. That was her story, and she was sticking to it.

Men were basically dogs, but women sometimes helped by wagging their tails just right.

Yet, here she found herself doing almost exactly that. Not that her sizing up Matt Rossi sexually happened in the first couple of seconds. Well, maybe. But she shouldn't be thinking of him in that way at all. There was nothing redeeming about him save his looks—that short, dark, mussed hair with those intense brown eyes—and she hated that this alone was enough to make her think lascivious thoughts.

Meg went for the mind. She didn't think about men that way until she found their brains sexy. That was her story, and she was sticking to it.

Until Rossi.

This was an aberration, she decided. One she could just brush aside. He might be intelligent, but in a really annoying way. His brain was *not* sexy. So being hot for that gorgeous body was a rare, stray, hormone-charged anomaly. That was her story and she was sticking to it.

"When you drop down from the clouds, let me know," she vaguely heard.

Meg shook her head and looked up. Tina was grinning. That was ominous. Tina never grinned unless she'd just kicked a guy between his rocks and his hard place.

"I was just thinking about a new plot twist," Meg said.

"Like doing it with the murder victim?"

"Tina—"

"Just an observation," Tina said, examining her nails.

"Well, observe something else."

"Like how gorgeous Mr. Murder is?"

"Is he? I hadn't noticed."

"Oh, good. Then you won't mind if I flirt with him a little."

"Do it and die, babe."

"Ha! I knew it!"

Meg was mortified at her knee-jerk reaction. "I'm just saying don't mess with the guests."

"Right."

"Do you want to mess with me right now? And I might mention I'm PMSing."

"I'm out of here."

"Good decision."

The problem was, Meg *wasn't* PMSing. Unless PMS stood for "Please, Matt, Sex." Which was dumb as dumb could be. Sure, he was good-looking. But he was also infuriating. The man had walked in and honestly believed he could take over. Just because he owned the place, he thought he could just waltz in and take control.

Control. That was the word. He was into control. Which made him so unappealing in the sexiest kind of way. Her father had been a control freak, too. Until her mother had died when Meg was ten, Jeanie Renshaw had been a buffer between father and children. But once she was gone the household had become a boot camp. And Meg had been the designated sergeant, being the eldest.

Learning to improvise had been so necessary. Checklists and protocols had become evil before she'd even turned into a teenager.

A rap on her office door brought her head up and her brain down from the clouds of memories. She looked at Mr. Checklist himself, standing in the doorway, busy scribbling notes on a legal pad. Great. More lists.

Meg took a moment to realize she didn't appear

all that professional in jeans and a Black Death European tour T-shirt. But they were under the gun and she had to be prepared to do anything from paperwork to housework.

She sighed. "Don't come in, Mr. Rossi."

"Too late," he said, strolling through the door.

She didn't think she could stuff that legal pad down his throat, but she'd love to give it a shot. "Look, you're the dead guy. You've got one major speech and then you're gone until you return as the ghost. From then on, you wing it. We've been through this."

"I think we should be caught making love before the murder."

Meg was *never* speechless. Right now her vocal chords had gone south. "Huh?" was about as much noise as she could conjure.

He looked at her with something very akin to pity. "You. Me. In bed."

She needed to swallow. In fact, breathing might be a good idea, too. Fantasizing was out of the question, even if her brain was malfunctioning and doing it anyway.

"I'm—" she kind of squeaked, then cleared her throat "—not sure why that's necessary."

"Because we're having an affair," he said, tapping his notes. "We need to be caught."

"I'm not certain that's necessary," she repeated. Although it sounded fun in theory.

He sighed and dropped his pad on the desk. "Do you want this weekend to be successful?"

"Well, yes."

"Then it needs to have a little 'oomph.'"

She swallowed. Hard. "Oomphing" sounded a little naughty. And nice.

"And you have to kill me."

"Excuse me?"

"You are my killer."

"The maid is your killer."

He looked utterly exasperated. Although he looked really good exasperated, she felt she should own that emotion at the moment. He was driving her nuts.

With the patience of a saint trying to reform a sinner, he said slowly, "What motivation does the maid have for murdering her boss? That puts her out of a job."

Talk about motivation. She was becoming more motivated by the moment to be his killer. "She's having an affair with one of the men that *you* are promising to ruin."

He shook his head. "Too many affairs happening. Just you and me."

Meg tossed down her pen. "Why don't you just rewrite the entire script?"

"As a matter of fact—"

Meg stood, knocking over her chair. "Stop right there. We are one day away from this production.

The actors all have their scripts. You're asking them to change at this point?"

"It's not a huge change."

"You're changing the murderer. That sounds pretty drastic to me."

"Wouldn't you like to kill me?" he asked, a twinkle in his brown eyes.

"Right now? Absolutely. And I'm a pacifist."

"Good. Then you won't have to fake it." He sat down and laid all of his notes between them, sideways. "Now here's how I see it…"

Meg looked down at a detailed checklist.

Murdering him was not going to be a problem.

MATT SPENT the rest of the day checking off, one-by-one, the items on his list. He knew Meg was seriously hacked off at him, but she'd surprised him by going with the flow. He knew if the situation were reversed, he'd be furious. He didn't like people changing his game plans. He also recognized he was doing exactly that to hers, and it was pretty intrusive. Unfortunately, it was just who he was.

Matt couldn't pinpoint exactly what explosive event in his life had turned him into the man he was now. Not that it mattered. So far almost every goal he'd ever set he'd accomplished. So that was a good thing, right?

Except he didn't feel triumphant about it all right now, and he didn't know why. Megan Renshaw was exactly the type of woman who drove him crazy. She let any change in plan roll right off her back. She didn't seem to care when things went wrong. She just amended her plans.

Take this morning, for instance. The cook had practically burned his kitchen down by experimenting with a flambé that obviously had a little too much fire power in it. Meg had walked in, calmly doused the flames with an extinguisher, then patted the woman and said, "It'll be better next time."

He'd about had a stroke. Meg sailed out of there as if the cook had simply put a little too much salt in the soup.

Matt had followed her, trying to keep from exploding. When he'd confronted her with "That woman is dangerous," all she'd done was smile and say "I'll keep an eye on her."

There was something about Meg that was dangerous, too. And it wasn't just that she found disasters amusing. Although that was part of it.

He wasn't accustomed to being *indulged*. He was accustomed to being listened to. Having his plans followed.

And while Meg seemed willing to follow his game plan to a certain extent, twice she'd looked at one of his proposed changes and just grinned and said, "That's cute. No."

But she *had* given in on his suggestion that her

character was having an affair with his character. He liked that. He wasn't so sure that he was as enthusiastic at her cheerful willingness to kill him.

5

REHEARSAL WAS TURNING OUT to be an utter disaster. In a kind of funny way, Meg decided. Maybe they could turn this into a comedy. As it was right now, it would be a mystery if it actually worked.

Lori Benedict, the actress playing the maid, Molly, was running her lines with all the enthusiasm of a convict being walked to the gas chamber. She had been really relishing her role as the murderer, especially when she took one look at the victim, and she wasn't happy with the change in plans.

The rest of the cast—which included the butler, three couples whose lives and livelihoods Lionel De Wynter would threaten to ruin, the homicide detective, Matt, and Meg—was still enthusiastic about the gig, but since so much of the script had changed, they were all a little confused.

Except for Rossi, of course, who'd studied his lines for about three and a half seconds before tossing down his script.

And although he was a godsend, his talent still

irritated Meg. And she wasn't quite sure why. Maybe because he kind of reminded her of Mike in a way. Mike, with his charm and looks and brains, seemed to have had it easy all of his life. He hadn't had to work too hard at anything.

Now she didn't know Matt well enough to make such a sweeping judgment about him like that, but so far he'd pretty much taken command without batting an eye, and had gotten his way with just about everything so far.

Even when she'd surprised him by agreeing to the plot twist that the two of them were having an affair, he'd just smiled as if she'd just dumped a floor full of Christmas presents under his tree.

She had drawn the line at the two of them getting caught in flagrante delicto, and he'd instantly erased the line, arguing that when suspicion was being cast her way, she could always protest that she had no motive, since she was madly in love with him.

"What is her motive?" the elegant elderly woman playing the better half of the Holmes family asked.

"He stinks in the sack," Meg whispered, for his ears only. The smile she shot him was pure innocence.

His, on the other hand, turned a tad feral. But then he faced the woman who'd asked and said, "After years of faithful service, he's about to terminate her both in the office and out. She's furious. Of course, none of you as guests will be aware of that. If you follow your scripts and hit your cues, the paying guests will have to puzzle it out. So absolutely no hints except the ones we *want* them to discover."

Meg crossed her arms at the "we" thing. She tried to think back on the exact moment she'd lost control of this weekend. As near as she could figure, it was the moment this man had stormed through the front door.

"Okay, folks, let's go through the dinner scene one more time," the idiot commanded. "You can use your scripts. But by tomorrow's run-through, know your lines. And remember your time lines."

Meg caught his eye and raised her brows.

He shrugged, then said with a slight smile, "Okay with you, boss?"

She had this fleeting need to overrule him, just for the sake of doing it, and to assert her authority to everyone in the room.

Unfortunately, her practical side said they needed to do exactly as he said. She just wished she'd said it first.

"One more thing," she said. "Remember that you aren't to acknowledge the guests in any way. As far as you're concerned, they're invisible."

"That seems kind of un-Southern," drawled the woman playing Agatha Bond, wife of Jim, the owner of a nationwide chain of bookstores. "We Southerners pride ourselves on our manners. You might not realize that, being a...you know."

The woman made it sound like a curse. Which was pretty good, considering Agatha hailed from Cleveland. Meg gave her brownie points for staying in character. "They're going to know you'll be pretending not to see them. They won't be upset."

"It's just...unseemly."

Okay, there was "in character" and there was annoying. "Not to worry," Meg said, "they're all from New York." They weren't. "They'll feel right at home."

Meg felt a boatload of satisfaction when she heard Rossi choke on his Coke.

"Why am I barging into the master bedroom an hour after supper now?" the man playing Watson Holmes asked. "I thought I was supposed to be rifling through the bast—er, the Lord of the Manor's desk then."

Meg jumped in before Matt could explain in lurid detail. "You're confronting him in a murderous rage. You're furious that he's just informed your wife that she either sells him her pipe and violin empire, or he'd see her go up in smoke, so to speak. But what you come upon is a little more interesting. You're going to share what you discover with your wife, but she's never been known to keep a secret, and will soon inform all of the other guests."

"What if I don't recognize what I'm supposed to find?"

"Oh, you'll recognize what it is right away," Tina said from the back of the parlor.

Meg shot Tina a dirty look over her shoulder. "Okay, one final full rehearsal, people. Our guests will be arriving in less than five hours."

THE FINAL REHEARSAL would have been a major success if Matt had been playing everyone's part. He had *all* the parts down. Without scripts the actors weren't all that impressive. But he was something to behold.

"Do you have your time lines down?" Rossi, who'd been amazingly non-dictatorlike during the initial run, asked.

A chorus of "yes" greeted him.

"All of you have your watches in sync?"

"Yes."

"Then let's get through it. Meg and butler to the entrance. Tina and guests to the cottage out back. Remember you won't be beginning to arrive until the paying guests are all in place."

Everyone began to file to their respective starting points. Meg took one look at Matt, knowing her eyes were slightly pathetically pleading.

He smiled, a stomach-melting smile that

burned straight up to her chest. "Of course it's going to be okay. You organized it, didn't you?"

She almost teared up at the thoughtful response. And felt he deserved one in return. "*We* organized it."

He winked at her. "Now if we can just keep the cook from burning down the place."

"Already taken care of," Meg said. "I recruited a local off-duty volunteer fireman to pretend to be her assistant chef."

He laughed, then bowed in his regal Lionel De Wynter fashion. Taking her hand, he planted a lingering kiss on her palm. "Why, my beautiful assistant and paramour, don't you think of everything?"

No, he was pretty certain she'd been honing in on just *one* thing. "Then why are you dumping me?" she asked, irrationally miffed he was, even if it wasn't real.

"Because you're lousy in the sack."

Plunging that fake knife into his heart was going to be a piece of chocolate cheesecake.

MEG PACED THE SALON, occasionally rubbing unusually sweaty palms against her prim and proper gray skirt. She pushed up the fake glasses on her nose, then checked her tight bun at the back of her neck. She'd had to pilfer a wig from Terence Brogan's Shakespeare collection, because her own hair wasn't long enough to pull it off.

Meg glanced in the mirror and groaned. She'd had to really shake out the wig to get rid of most of the powder. But she still looked like an old frump.

This was good for the play, not exactly good for her self-esteem. Although she was no beauty by a long shot, she still didn't relish Matt seeing her in all her ugly glory.

When had she even given a second thought to her looks? Well, for her wedding day, she supposed. But that had been girlish foolishness. Wanting to look like a princess for your soon-to-be husband was natural for a kid who'd still had mega stars in her eyes. But since then, as long as she didn't send clients screaming down a dark alley into the night to get away from her, who cared?

And how was *anyone* going to believe that a hunk like Lionel De Wynter would willingly climb into bed with her?

After she'd dressed earlier, she'd called him on his cell phone and voiced her concerns. He'd said, "Trust me, I've got a trick up my sleeve."

"Since when did you turn magician, frat boy?" she'd said.

"When I met you." And with that he'd disconnected without any parting words whatsoever.

6

ALL WAS SET. The tourists were in place in the salon and Tina had advised them they were invisible. That would be a good thing if Mr. Hopkins wasn't wearing enough cologne to choke an elephant and Mrs. Warner didn't snap her gum loud enough to cause avalanches.

Worst of all, Mr. Danks's "wife" wasn't even human. She was a Persian feline named Fluffy. Apparently Fluffy was his good luck charm. And Meg had forgotten to stipulate that animals weren't invited. When Tina tried to gently suggest Fluffy be sent to a kennel for a couple of days, Mr. Danks about had a stroke.

He pulled out a wad of bills. "How much to keep her with me? I can't think without Fluffy."

Molly the Maid saw all that cash, and immediately sidled closer to the man. This was not in the script. And the gleam in her eyes didn't appear to be acting.

But then the gleam turned watery, and she

started sneezing. Molly the Maid was apparently allergic to felines.

Tina glanced at Meg, who shook her head. "No extra charge, Mr. Danks," Tina said. "Fluffy's welcome. But we don't have any cat food or litter."

"Not a problem," he said, cuddling his kitty. "I brought everything she needs."

THE GUESTS WERE THERE, the players were there, except for Matt.

One by one the three acting couples entered the salon, each thankfully sticking to their scripts and ignoring the amateur sleuths.

Meg introduced herself. "I'm Madeline Hatter, Mr. De Wynter's personal assistant. Thank you all for coming. Please get comfortable, and refreshments will be along shortly." Meg pried Molly the Maid off Mr. Danks and directed her to bring in the hors d'oeuvres and wine.

"Ms. Hatter, can you give us a hint as to why Mr. De Wynter has summoned us here tonight?" Jim Bond, publishing mogul, asked.

"I couldn't say," Meg said.

"Or you won't," said his wife, Agatha.

"As you wish," said Meg, which she knew wasn't the right line, but nerves were getting to her. She *was not* an actress.

"I'll tell you why," intoned a somewhat drunken male voice behind them.

Meg whirled to see Terence Brogan standing there, looking like a disheveled Hamlet, in tights and a tunic.

Rushing over to him, Meg said, "I think we should let Mr. De Wynter explain his intentions."

"My dear lady," he said, then wiped the dribble from his lips. "I *am* Mr. De Wynter."

Meg turned to the guests with a nervous giggle. "I'm sorry, folks. I'd forgotten that Mr. De Wynter's twin brother was visiting for the weekend." She made a circling motion at her temple and shrugged sheepishly. Grabbing his arm, she said, "Russell, you know you shouldn't be out of bed. You are recuperating."

"The show must go on," he slurred.

"What the devil is going on here?" Matt said.

Meg turned to him trying not to look panicked. "I'm sorry, sir, your *brother* seems to have wandered from his sick bed."

"My bro—"

"Yes. He's not listening to doctor's orders. I think maybe you need to have Jeeves get him back to his room."

Even in the middle of a mini-disaster, Meg had time to appreciate Matthew Rossi in a smoking jacket. He looked phenomenally sexy, aristocratic and villainous. He was even puffing on a pipe, a prop he'd come up with all on his own.

"The two of them are twins?" Meg heard

Tammy Warner whisper. She couldn't blame the woman. Matt looked *maybe* mid-thirties. Mr. Brogan was easily sixty. Matt probably would look sexy as sin in tights. Mr. Brogan, well, was no Mel Gibson.

Puff, puff. "I see," Matt said. "Yes, we need to get..."

"Russell."

"Yes, Russell back into bed. We wouldn't want to have..."

"A relapse."

"Yes, a relapse." He nodded imperiously. "Ring for Jeeves, please, Miss Hatter."

"Who is this imposter?" Brogan asked, hiking a thumb at Matt.

"Jeeves!" Meg practically screeched.

"The bell pull, Miss Hatter," Matt advised, not missing an acting beat.

She'd play along if she knew what a bell pull *was*.

He cocked his head toward a burgundy rope with a big knot on the end.

Meg trotted over to it and started pulling like crazy.

"Once is sufficient, Miss Hatter," Matt said, in an irritatingly smug tone.

She let go of the rope. "I hear you say that a lot, sir."

Matt's eyes narrowed. Luckily, Jeeves showed up just in time. "Sir?"

"Take my brother...er—"

"Russell," Meg reminded him.

"Russell, right. Take Russell back to his room and see that he's comfortable. Make certain he takes his medication. In fact, you might want to double the dose. He seems in extraordinary pain."

"I'm out of medication," Brogan said. "And let me tell you—"

"Then give him some of Glenda's special cocoa," Meg jumped in. There'd be enough Kahlúa in it to put the man out for the night.

It was a bit of a struggle, but Jeeves finally managed to wrestle Brogan from the room.

When all settled down, Matt greeted his fake guests. It was almost funny to watch all the real guests writing down notes as if they were going to be quizzed later.

"You might be wondering why I've asked you all here," Matt said in his condescending De Wynter voice. "Well, let me put the mystery to rest. I'm about to put you all out of business. Dinner, everyone?"

"THAT WAS GREAT!" Meg said, bouncing her butt on Matt's bed. "That was great!"

Matt's De Wynter mask melted away and he became stuffy entrepreneur once again. "Which part? Where Brogan invaded the party or when Molly deliberately spilled Mr. Danks's wine all over his lap?"

Meg waved. "Who cares? They were having fun, scribbling notes and whispering to each other."

"Everyone was ad-libbing," he further complained.

"So what?"

"They should have known their lines." He tossed off his smoking jacket, leaving him in navy silk pajamas that were made for him.

Meg was in danger of drooling as much as poor Mr. Brogan. "You can't ask them to learn an entire new script overnight. It worked out just fine."

"I've never had rice pilaf made with booze before."

Meg stood and plunked her hands on her hips. "Anyone ever tell you that you're pretty annoying?"

He dropped his pipe on the marble dressing table, then turned back to her. "There's nothing wrong with expecting an agenda to be followed."

Meg counted to ten. "The guests had fun. The basic stage is set. Chill out already."

He stalked over to her, his brown eyes burning. "How have you survived so long 'chilling out'? How have you kept this job?"

She pulled off her wig and shook out her hair. "How have you existed living by damn lists? You know, they're really irritating. Don't you ever just sit back and let things happen?"

"Never."

"I find that sad."

He took another step closer, within cologne sniffing and body heat range. Meg would have stepped back except she liked his cologne and his body heat.

"Ms. Renshaw, I haven't gotten where I have in life by letting fate rule me. I rule my fate. And I like it that way. So please save your pity for someone who needs it."

Oh, she didn't pity him. Well, maybe a little. Of course she admired the man's success. But to her way of thinking, it had come at a really high price.

She sniffed. "I'd ask where this all started, but I really don't care. Just play your part and let's get this over with. Then you can go back to making all of those hoity-toity lists you're so fond of."

He actually smiled. "Well, then, get changed for our next act, Ms. Hatter. Your negligee is in my closet. I picked it out myself."

Meg was beginning to regret taking his bait and writing in the affair part. She swallowed. Hard. "Maybe we should improvise that part?"

He shook his head and his killer smile grew wider. "Integral to the plot."

She gulped. "How about if we're just caught kissing standing up?"

"How undramatic would that be? Besides, they have to catch us in a very compromising position. It's important."

He had dazzling white teeth. And a really

handsome face. But his close proximity and body heat were becoming uncomfortable. "We could just be caught talking dirty or something."

"That's not how you wrote it," he said.

"Ha! You egged me into that."

"You bet your sweet lips I did." He checked his watch. "Now hurry up. We have to be making love in twenty-three minutes."

7

When Matt had gone out earlier in the afternoon to secure the props he'd wanted for his character, he'd happened to pass a lingerie store in the mall. It hadn't been on his list to obtain an outfit for Meg, but once the idea had planted itself in his mind, he mentally added it as a "must do."

The emerald negligee had caught his eye instantly, because all he could think about was what it would do to her eyes. Not that it should matter. They were just playing a part. But what the heck, she might as well look stunning so he could really get into his role.

Smart move. She looked stunning, all right. Embarrassed, too, which made no sense because with the flowing robe overtop of the nightgown itself, very little flesh was showing.

Too bad.

He had to keep himself from whistling.

Then again, she looked as if she wanted to keep herself from socking him. "I don't understand this. I'm supposed to be dowdy."

Matt stacked his hands behind his head as he lounged on the king-size bed. "No, you're supposed to be outwardly dowdy. Now they're going to discover you aren't who they think you are."

"They're going to think I'm a cheap floozy," she said, eyes flashing gorgeously.

"A floozy, maybe, but not cheap." No kidding. She looked like a million bucks. And he'd like to deposit every single dollar bill in his account, so to speak.

Matt swallowed hard at that thought. A woman like Megan Renshaw most definitely didn't figure into his plans. Not that she'd shown any inclination to make his "to do" list, but still, finding her attractive was a bad idea.

It was hard to deny, though, that her skin looked good enough to lick all night long. It glowed under the chandelier like cream. Her hair was tousled from the way she'd flung off that hideous wig, and her lips appeared ripe and swollen, probably from biting them as she'd held back swearwords while donning the negligee.

Her lips suddenly turned up, and she held up a hand like a student in a classroom. "I know! We'll just have one of the actors let it drop that he or she had just caught us in a...delicate situation."

That idea didn't appeal for some reason. "No, I don't think so," he said, sitting up straighter.

"The guests might think it's a red herring clue. This has to be more realistic. They have to *see* it."

She blew an exasperated breath. "You're an exhibitionist, aren't you?"

He almost laughed. "Not that I'm aware."

"Well, you're enjoying this too much."

Yes, indeed, he was. "You rewrote the script, darling."

"Don't call me darling." Meg tried to straighten her hair. "Besides, you practically dared me."

Practically? Now that he thought about it, he'd set the trap. Now he felt a little like a rat. He was used to manipulating people in business, but she was an innocent in the scheme of things. He didn't take advantage of innocents. No matter how much he wanted to play out this scene, it didn't seem fair, and she looked really reluctant. With regret weighing down his gut, he sighed. "Look, if you really don't want to—"

The intercom squawked. "The troops are heading your way. Places everyone."

They stared at each other. Matt felt the call of her eyes and said again softly, "If you don't want to—"

Before he could finish the sentence, she threw off the robe and practically dove into the bed. "Pucker up, lover."

MEG WASN'T PREPARED for Matt's pucker. She wasn't prepared for the firmness of his lips, or the way they moved over hers as if the two of them had been doing this for years.

Mostly, though, she wasn't prepared for his hands on her body. He could give lessons in acting like a lover.

He'd rolled her over so that he was sprawled all over her, but he kept most of the weight on his arms to keep from crushing her. She thought that was cute and thoughtful and sexy all at once.

Then she stopped thinking. Feeling was good enough.

Matt stroked her face, from ears to temples. He took turns kissing her mouth, her cheeks, her neck. He licked and nipped and sucked with total abandon. Meg had never felt so ravished and so happy.

The greatest feeling, though, came from the rest of his body. If it was acting along with him, it was giving an award-winning performance.

Meg forgot all about *why* she was doing this and only knew why she didn't want it to end. It took a long time for the whispers to register, only after Matt's lips moved back to her ear and he whispered, "We have company, babe."

She stiffened, but he didn't miss a beat. "Relax, love," he said, loud enough for their company to hear them. "No one knows you're still here."

Meg was pretty sure she had a line for that comment, but for the life of her, she couldn't remember what it was supposed to be.

Through a fog she heard a cat hiss, a person sneeze and someone say, "Who is that woman he's with?"

Another sneeze, and then Molly the Maid said, her voice sounding a little nasal, "That's his assistant, of course."

What do you know, Molly remembered a line.

"He's been boffing her for years."

That wasn't in the script. Meg almost choked. And the entire situation hit her. She was lying here in sexy night attire, making out with a stranger in front of witnesses. And until this moment all she'd been thinking about was the making out part.

She began to wiggle under him, but he held her firm. "Stay in character, sweet pea," Matt growled into her ear.

"Get bent," she whispered back.

"Say your line," he reminded her.

Meg dug through her memory. Oh, yeah. "Lionel, darling, do you think it was wise to threaten all of those people tonight?"

"Threaten? I didn't threaten, love. I promised."

"They were very upset."

"As well they should be. It's not pretty being stupid."

"But Mrs. Holmes was threatening to sue. Or worse."

"Let her try."

"Mr. Drew said he'd see you in hell first."

"At least I'll beat him there."

Meg forgot her next line. Mostly because she was concentrating more on his lips than her dialogue. He noticed, too, and smiled. "Yes, my darling personal assistant, save me from hell and take me to heaven instead."

That hadn't been in the script.

Meg found herself admiring his improvisational skills.

It took the guests around ten interminable minutes to whisper among themselves, then scribble furiously. It wasn't that Matt was averse to keeping up the pretense of a torrid affair, but doing it in front of onlookers was definitely making Meg uncomfortable. And although she worked it like a trouper, even improvising a few bite marks to his neck and some nibbling on his ear, he could tell by the stiffness in her body that she wasn't used to voyeurism as a rule.

Not that he was, either, but heck, why not submerge yourself in a role?

When everyone had finally left the master bedroom, Meg shot off the bed as if it were radioactive. Her cheeks were blooming with color, and her breathing was coming out in wispy gasps.

She was gorgeous when she was mortified.

If he weren't a gentleman, he'd mortify her more often.

Matt nearly choked on the thought. He was keenly aware that his body was pulsing and his blood pressure was probably through the roof. Not that it was such a surprise.

The woman was deadly gorgeous. A man would have to be a eunuch not to respond to those lips and those big gray eyes. Not to mention the curves. In business attire she looked kind of skinny, but looks could be deceiving. She had plenty of shape. Plenty.

"You took that a little far, don't you think?" she rasped.

"Just playing the part," he lied outrageously.

"Yes, well…" she stammered.

"Okay, next up," he said, checking his watch, which wasn't a real good distraction from Meg Renshaw in a negligee, but he gave it the old college try, "the maid returns in about two hours to find me dead." He prudently decided not to point out that that was plenty of time for them to complete the illusion that they were, in fact, lovers.

Meg nodded as she gathered up her scattered clothing. "I need to get out of the house so I can come in after the reveal."

"How are you going to get out without anyone seeing you?"

"The secret passageway, of course."

"Secret passageway?"

"Oh, come on. You own this house. How could you not know about the secret passageways?"

"Of course I do," he said, then ran a hand through his hair. "No, I don't."

She peered at him, hugging her frumpy clothes to her chest. "You bought this house why?"

Matt shrugged. "I wanted lots of space for my family."

Her mouth dropped open. "You're *married?*" she squeaked.

The horror on her face would have been priceless if he'd wanted her to be horrified, which he didn't. "No. No, I'm not married. I mean my future family."

"Are you engaged?"

"No."

"Dating?"

"Not right this minute."

"But you have a girlfriend."

He was beginning to feel like he was in a congressional probe. "No, not right this minute."

Her wide eyes narrowed. "Oh, I see. You have it all planned out, right?"

Now she was getting the point. "Next on my list."

For some reason she doubled over. He panicked for a moment before he realized her body was shaking from laughter, not a seizure. "What's so funny about that?" he asked, a little disappointed that she had clothes covering her chest when he might have caught a tiny glimpse of heaven.

It took her longer than it should to compose

herself, stop shaking and straighten. "You are some piece of work, Mr. Rossi."

He didn't want to know what she meant by that. "What's that supposed to mean?"

She shook her head and swiped at her eyes. "You don't want to know."

No, he didn't. "Yes, I do."

Meg tried to stifle her grin, but she was doing a lousy job of it. "I just don't understand people like you. How boring it must be to follow a strict game plan."

Boring! Who was she to call him boring? He crossed his arms. "Strictly following a game plan is what made me rich."

Her nose wrinkled. "As in money? Big deal."

"What other kind of rich is there?" he asked, figuring it was probably a stupid question, but he was truly curious.

Her snort wasn't exactly ladylike. "If you have to ask, it's useless even trying to explain."

Well, that wasn't exactly helpful. "If you think rich involves flying by the seat of your pants, no thanks."

She turned and headed for the bathroom. "I'm changing now."

"Need help?"

"No, thanks. I'm sure helping me dress isn't on your list."

"I'll add it," he said, only half joking.

"No, thanks," she repeated. But he could swear he heard her mutter, "What an idiot," right before the bathroom door slammed shut.

MEG GRIMACED at her clothes in distaste as she shoved them on her body. She had no idea why she hated looking so bad. After all, there certainly wasn't anyone here she wanted to impress. Definitely *not* Dudley Do-List.

"Is there an entrance to the secret passageway from this room?" Matt called through the door.

"Yes."

There was a moment of silence. Finally, he said, "Well?"

"Well what?"

"Where is it?"

Meg grinned. "See if you can't find it yourself, Sherlock."

After all, it had taken her almost a half hour to find it herself, and that was *with* the house plans in her hands. "Let's just see how smart you really are, Mr. Rossi," she whispered to herself. Then she took a final look in the mirror, stuck her tongue out at the image peering back at her and walked out of the bathroom.

8

WHEN MEG EMERGED from the bathroom she had to stifle a snort of laughter. Matt was busy trying to move every brick in the fireplace. Then he began lifting all of the knickknacks on the mantel. Then he tried to take the beveled mirror down, but it was bolted to the wall.

"Cold," Meg said.

He turned abruptly, and his neck got a little red. "Excuse me?"

"You're cold. Not even close."

He took one step toward the left.

"Colder."

He took two steps toward the right.

"Getting warmer."

He stopped in front of a portrait of a man dressed in period attire and sporting a handlebar mustache. Meg didn't know if the man in the painting was the original owner of the house, but if he was, his wife might have just done the world a favor because the man had really beady eyes.

Testing out the possibilities, Matt finally swung the portrait to his left and uncovered a wall safe. He turned to Meg with a triumphant look that would have been amusing if he didn't look good enough to eat.

Meg crossed her arms. "That safe is...what? Two feet by three feet? You think you'll find your hidden passage behind it?"

He scowled, and amazingly *still* looked good enough to eat. "No, but it might hide the button or knob or whatever that reveals the passageway."

"You might be warmer, but you're still in the fridge, buddy."

He frowned even more. "I've never seen anything like this. There are just four buttons here."

"Different, isn't it?"

"Only four buttons titled Harry, Moe, Curly and Sheep?"

"To ward off copyright infringement, I'm guessing."

He looked at her strangely, but then turned back to the safe. "What are you supposed to do?"

"Press the buttons in the correct order. It's like a button combination."

"Okay. So what's the combination?"

"Figure it out."

His face was getting redder by the nanosecond. "Is ringing a woman's neck in total aggravation a reasonable defense in a homicide?"

"I don't think so." *I hope.*

"You better hope not. Tell me now, I own this house."

"No."

He glared at her. And she could *still* gobble him up. "I'm beginning not to like you, Ms. Renshaw."

"Just now? And here I began that process the moment you walked in the door."

"I've been nothing but—"

"Obnoxious, overbearing, demanding. Pick a word."

"I was going for gracious. Possibly helpful."

"Ha!" But then it occurred to her that he'd actually been both, even if it soured her tummy to realize it. "Okay, you're not *too* bad."

"I'm also cute."

"Don't push it." Sighing dramatically, just for effect, she said, "You don't know your Three Stooges, do you, Mr. Rossi?"

He tossed her a smile that would have melted an iceberg. She made a conscious decision to make herself melt-proof.

After all, he'd kissed her like he meant to. *Now* he didn't like her? A girl could definitely take offense.

The man stared at the safe for a while. "Sheep is the wrong answer. It's between the other three."

"Unless they're throwing you off. Everything tonight depends on that safe."

"You didn't write this in the script."

"Of course not! It's a mystery."

"And you're counting on sheep?"

"I'm counting on them." She smiled. "That's the best clue you're getting."

"I'm in the play, I should know the ending."

"I know. So should I."

From the walkie-talkie, they heard Tina squawk, "My life is over! This is a disaster. My life is over."

Matt looked over at Meg, one brow raised.

"She probably broke a fingernail."

AMAZINGLY, Meg had been right. Tina had broken a fingernail. Matt had met drama queens before, but Tina was setting records.

Meg had disappeared for about five minutes, then returned. "All's well."

"You regrew her nail for her?"

"Something like that."

He waited for more, but should have expected she'd leave it at that. He'd known her for all of three days, but in that time it had become abundantly clear that Megan Renshaw took catastrophe in stride.

He couldn't imagine how anyone could live that way, but hey, if it worked for her, who was he to judge? Besides, she'd be out of his life soon enough.

For some reason that wasn't exactly a cheery thought. He should be glad to be rid of her and her band of Looney Tunes. For sure he was firing his estate manager. No more murders, real or faked, were going to happen in his family's home.

If he ever *got* a family.

Well, it wasn't a matter of *if* exactly, but *when*. After all, it was on his list, and so far everything he'd ever placed on his list he achieved eventually.

Sluffing off the niggling pinch of possible failure, Matt leafed through the scene of Molly the Maid bringing him all the lovely things he was going to show his guests, but he was fuming at the head of this operation, suddenly. He wanted to hate her, sue her, punish her for messing with his plans, but instead all he wanted was to lie back down on the bed with her.

Dumb, dumb, dumb.

After all, he was getting a little tired of her thinking he was a stick-in-the-mud. He'd love to prove her wrong. But he didn't know how.

He tossed down the Molly Maid scene and stalked back over to the wall safe. "Combination?"

She laughed. "There are only four buttons. You haven't figured it out yet?"

"I didn't try." *Much.*

"Did you try just pulling on the latch?"

"Huh?"

"It's not locked."

Matt turned back to the safe and yanked. Sure enough, it opened. "There are jewels in here!"

"Paste."

He turned slowly, a glittering faux diamond necklace in his hand. "And you know this how?"

"I double as a jewel thief at night."

A grin tugged at Matt's lips, but Meg could tell he was trying very hard to look annoyed. "Wouldn't surprise me."

"Let me save you a little time here. There is no magic button in there that will lead you to the passageway."

Matt tossed the necklace back into the safe and returned the portrait of mustache man to its place.

He turned to his right again. "Point me in the general direction."

"You know, you're not much fun."

"I'm a stand-up comedian at night. Point."

Meg sighed. She fluttered her fingers. "Walk-in closet."

She watched, amused, while Matt strode to the closet, determination making his butt look cute.

Actually, he didn't need determination to make his butt look cute.

Actually, she shouldn't be making observations about his butt.

Actually, she probably shouldn't even be looking at his butt.

But what the hell? The job had perks and she didn't see any reason not to enjoy them.

Except he turned abruptly at the door to the

closet and caught her in mid-ogle. "Something wrong?" he asked, brows raised.

Yes. He'd caught her. "I was trying to decide what color those pajamas are."

He looked down. "Just a guess, but I'd say blue."

As opposed to, say, her face, which was probably fire-engine red. "I meant what shade of blue, exactly."

He had the decency not to smirk. "I think they call it 'cheeky blue.'"

Meg crossed her arms over her chest. "So I was looking at your behind. So what?"

"So nothing. I'm flattered."

Dignity was a fleeting thing. "Who says I liked what I saw?"

"Who says you didn't?"

Not her. "Find the passageway already. I'm getting bored." Not to mention a little hot around the collar.

MATT FELT a strange elation. Meg had liked what she'd seen, whether she admitted it or not. Why that made him happy, he wasn't sure, and he didn't think that was an avenue he wanted to explore.

Unfortunately, there were plenty of avenues he really wanted to explore. Like the way to a naked Meg, for example.

But of course he was more mature than that. Sort

of. He might be in the market for a lifelong partner, but that didn't mean he couldn't have a fling.

And she kissed good. He could handle a few more of those. Just for fling purposes, of course. And practice. Face it, he hadn't had a girlfriend in years. He'd been a football player and golfer most of his life. He knew the importance of practice.

Then again, he also knew the importance of sanity. And he was uncomfortably close to feeling as if he was on the brink of losing his.

No, a naked Meg was a bad idea. Well, it was a really good visual, but still, all in all, a very bad idea.

Unless she really, really wanted to get naked for him. After all, his father had always told him to give a lady what she wants.

Matt shook his head. Definitely, he was verging on unbalanced.

Pulling open the gilded double doors, Matt strode into a closet that was easily as big as the living room in his old family home. Not that he didn't believe in getting used to luxury, but there was comfort and there was excess.

He flicked on the light switch, and the closet was bathed in a soft ambient light from…a crystal chandelier?

He stared up at it, then glanced over his shoulder at Meg. "Naturally, every closet should have one."

She wrinkled her nose. "It *is* a little pretentious, isn't it?"

"When I make renovations, that puppy is the first thing coming down."

"You can donate it to Goodwill."

He couldn't help but chuckle. "I'm sure there's a big market for them."

Although he was proud that he'd be able to provide well for his family, he also never wanted to instill in them a sense of entitlement.

His parents had worked their fingers to the bone, and so had he. His kids weren't getting any kind of free pass. He envisioned his sons, and maybe even his daughters, working as carpenters or in some such jobs in the summers, helping to renovate homes, just as he had done.

In fact, he kind of missed the hands-on, hard, backbreaking work and the satisfaction that came from watching his toil turn something ugly into something beautiful.

Enough about that. He had a passageway to find, and he was going to be a little embarrassed if he couldn't find it.

The closet wasn't packed with glittering clothes, but it had a fairly healthy array of suits, tuxes, casual clothes and silk pajamas. Get rid of the suits, tuxes and casual clothes and he could very well be standing in Hefner's place.

He looked around, trying to detect any telltale seams in the floor and walls. Nothing.

There was a floor-to-ceiling recessed mirror at

the far end of the closet. "Ah, ha!" he said, then strolled over to it, felt around the outer rim, thumped a few boards on either side, but still nothing.

He turned and looked around some more, avoiding the smile that was playing around Meg's mouth.

"Another hint?"

"Just a little one," he conceded, because they didn't have all night.

"Think Rube Goldberg."

"Oh, jeez."

He strolled around slowly, coming upon an electronic tie caddy. "I had one of these once," he murmured. "Damn thing never worked."

He pulled the chain, and sure enough, the supposedly rotating caddy just sat there. But to his astonishment, some invisible strings whisked clothes aside to reveal a wooden shoe shelf filled top to bottom with at least one hundred shoes.

He glanced at Meg, shooting her a smile of victory.

"Don't celebrate too soon," she said. "That's just step one."

Matt felt all around the shelf, but nothing. Then he stepped back and muttered, "What am I missing?"

"Well—"

"No. Not yet."

He looked for anything out of place. Basically,

it could have been a Gucci, Armani and Ferragamo smorgasbord. But then his eyes lit on a pair of cheap-looking penny loafers that he'd bet weren't even real leather. Feeling into the space, all he encountered was what seemed to be a tiny coin slot.

He looked down at the shoes again. "You've got to be kidding me."

Meg kept her silence.

Matt dug into one of the shoes and pulled out the shiny copper disk. Then he felt around until he located the slot, and shoved the coin into it. Disappointment clogged his gut when the penny wouldn't fall through all the way.

He stepped back, but then to his astonishment, the shoe rack parted like the Red Sea. "Well, I'll be damned," he said, staring into the black abyss beyond.

"Put the coin back in the shoe," Meg said. "And put them back."

He did as he was told, then turned abruptly, impetuously grabbing and hugging her. "I did it!"

She laughed up at him. "You certainly did."

His eyes narrowed. "How long did it take you?"

"Oh, much longer than that," she said.

He had the feeling she was just trying to salvage his pride, but at the moment he didn't care. She felt so good in his arms, and he wanted to kiss her. "What now?" he asked, his voice a little gravelly.

"We…uh, explore the passageway?"

He sort of liked that she put that in the form of a question. It left open other possibilities.

Matt checked his watch. "Probably not time right now. We have to get me ready to be murdered."

Her eyes took on a wicked light. "*Now* the good times are starting to roll."

"A guy could develop a complex," he said, but he let her go.

She showed him how to close the passageway again, and they returned to the bedroom suite.

"Let's check the weapon," Meg said.

"Bloodthirsty little wench, aren't you?"

She smiled. "You betcha."

9

MEGAN PULLED A GUN from a hidden drawer in the vanity near the windows flanking the left side of the bed. She checked it over very carefully as she strolled toward Matt.

By the look on his face he wasn't crazy about guns. When she stood about four feet in front of him, she aimed.

"Whoa, wait a minute."

"Relax, you'll only feel it for a second," she said, and aimed straight at his heart.

"Meg…"

She fired, and he flinched. Then he stared down in horror at his chest, which was now soaking wet with…water.

"Hey, that thing looks a little too real," he said, after a deep breath.

"Realism is the key," she said, pretending to holster it.

"That wasn't funny."

She blew out her lower lip. "Do I look like a homicidal maniac to you?"

"You knew how to handle and aim that gun pretty expertly."

She laughed. "I took advanced water pistol in phys. ed."

He rubbed at his chest as if he'd been mortally wounded.

Meg suddenly felt guilty. It never even occurred to her that she'd actually alarm him. But kids had been shot for cheaper-looking water pistols than this, so she couldn't blame him. "I'm sorry. I really am. I just figured you'd know it's too early to kill you off."

"You're a real card."

"Now for the blood."

"Oh, goody."

MEG SAT BEHIND the one-way mirror in the passageway, and watched the events in the murder of Lionel De Wynter unfold with amusement and a crazy admiration.

Everything was going wrong in the best possible way. *No one* would ever figure this one out. Because *no one* knew what they were doing.

One by one the couples playing the incensed entrepreneurs demanded an audience of Mr. De Wynter, and one by one they all forgot what their businesses were.

Matt ad-libbed like a champ, reminding Reed

and Chancy Drew that it was their gumball business he was after, not the lingerie sweatshop.

"But you want that lingerie," Reed accused.

"My girlfriends already own the best," Matt said. "None of which carry your label."

Some of the guests had chosen to follow this couple, some were following other events. With walkie-talkies, Tina and Timmy and Meg were keeping each other informed where everyone was.

The actress playing the part of Sherrie Holmes, married to Watson, the pipe and violin maker, decided to improvise that she was a past lover of Mr. De Wynter, and that was why he was trying to ruin them now.

Not in the script, people.

But the actress seemed to enjoy the idea of throwing herself at Lionel, who seemed to be enjoying it too much as well, which he'd hear about later. But Meg felt a certain giddiness when Lionel informed her that she no longer smoked his pipe.

Guests scribbled.

Jim and Agatha Bond, both faking British accents, said they would see his head hanging on a pike at the Tower of London before he'd take over their publishing company.

This wasn't in the script. It wasn't in any script Meg had ever heard of.

"Please forgive my great-great grandfather,

Lord and Lady Bond," Lionel/Rossi, who looked
about as British as a bulldog looked like a poodle,
said. "But he takes offense when his heirs are
threatened. Very definitely at the hands of barbar-
ians at the Tower. After all, his father's head was
displayed along the Thames for amusement and
fear, and he didn't much appreciate it."

Matt sighed and puffed on his pipe, choking
along the way, but covering it up with coughs of
disdain. "My ancestor made his way to this lovely
land, and built this magnificent home."

This. Is. Not. In. The. Script.

Meg wondered if her water pistol handled real
bullets.

LIONEL DE WYNTER died at midnight. Unfortunately, soaked in fake blood.

Meg couldn't figure out why she was angry.
He'd been superb. He had just done everything *his*
way. Without telling her. She didn't mind improvisation. But she did by a guy who seemed to want
to improvise without her consent.

And wasn't he Mr. Lists, after all? He'd made
her form lists for two days, and now he was just
going with the flow.

She wouldn't care, because it was going so well,
even if they were flying by the seat of their water
pistols.

But now it was her turn. He was dead, she was

back on the scene, and back in control. Because the man couldn't speak.

Perfect.

Meg watched as the guests went over Matt's body with a fine-tooth comb. She wondered how long he could not breathe.

Not that she cared but... She burst through the walk-in closet and said, "I did it!"

"She did it?"

"No, she couldn't have done it. She was in love with him."

"But if he was going to dump her..."

"Get out!" Meg shouted. "All of you get out, now! You can view the corpse later."

"But—"

"Molly, get them out now."

Molly sneezed her way out as she herded the troops.

"Matt, are you okay?" Meg asked in a whisper.

No answer.

"Matt, breathe!"

She pushed at his chest, begged to the Almighty, then shook him a little. Nothing roused him.

Trying to mine her brain for details of her first-aid education, she leaned his head back, pinched his nose and began blowing air into his lungs.

She stopped blowing when she felt his lips dip up in a smile.

Sitting back on her haunches, she glared down at him. "You were faking it!"

His eyes opened slowly and sparkled with life. "Of course I was faking it. I'm supposed to be dead."

"You jerk!" Meg scrambled off the bed and stood, assessing the room for any potential weapon.

Matt rose up onto his elbows. "Hey, I was just doing my job."

She smacked his thigh. "You didn't have to make it look so real."

"Don't tell me you were worried about me."

Her cheeks went into high burner mode. "Of course I was. I'd actually have to pay to have your carcass hauled off."

He grinned. "You were worried."

"You didn't have to make it look so real." She sounded sulky even to her own ears.

Matt reached for her arm and dragged her down onto the bed. "I'm sorry."

"Like hell."

"No, really, I am." He began caressing the soft side of her forearm. "I didn't mean to scare you."

That stroking motion on her skin was beginning to feel too good, so she pulled her hand back. Then regretted it immediately.

"So what do we do now, boss lady?" he asked.

And then it finally hit her that she'd just blown the whole mystery thing. Who was this man who could make her forget her entire reason for living?

She really, really didn't like what that said about her. Or him. Or them.

She thought about it for a moment, then smiled.

"Uh-oh," he said. "That smile is scary as hell. What do you have in mind?"

"I'm just going to have to kill you again."

10

MEG BREEZED INTO the library, a bright smile on her face. "Mr. De Wynter is going to be fine. He accidentally nicked himself with his razor."

"He looked dead to me," Lola Hopkins whispered to her husband.

Since Meg wasn't supposed to acknowledge the paying guests, she turned to Watson Holmes. "My goodness, he didn't look dead to you, did he?"

Holmes removed the pipe from his mouth. "He looked like he'd fainted. Not that I would be crying if he were dead."

Bless the man. Figured out right off the bat that the script hadn't just changed, it had flown straight out the window.

"Not to worry, Mr. De Wynter will be down shortly. He's just trying to pull himself together after passing out at the sight of his own blood."

The paying guests scribbled, Molly the Maid sneezed and Meg heard a barely concealed growl coming from her walkie-talkie.

Remembering that Matt was listening in for cues, Meg decided to enjoy the moment. "He likes to play the tough guy, but really he's a wimp at heart."

She covered the receiver to keep the guests from hearing Matt's response to that. "Truth to tell," she said, "he's not even that good in bed."

No amount of receiver-covering could muffle the "Miss Hatter!" yelled into the walkie-talkie. Cast, crew and guests all jumped at the same time.

Meg offered an apologetic smile then said into the phone, "Feeling better, Mr. De Wynter?" This role was getting more thrilling by the moment.

"Get your fanny up here, now," he growled.

"Oh, you must be recovering, sir," she said sweetly.

"Up here. Now."

Meg smiled at the actors. "Excuse me, please."

The paying guests scurried to follow her, which wasn't exactly a good thing.

But she couldn't very well tell them to stay behind when they were under the assumption this was all part of the plot. Little did they know the plot had gone to hell long ago.

As they ascended the steps, Meg spoke into the walkie-talkie. "We're heading up there right now," Meg said, hoping he'd get a clue and the guests didn't have one.

"Well, hurry up about it."

Meg finally acknowledged the guests. "What a

grump. I wonder if anyone would testify against me if a gun I happen to be carrying accidentally went off?"

"Not me," said Mrs. Hopkins.

"Achoo!" said Molly the Maid.

They made their way up to the third floor and the master bedroom. Meg crossed her fingers and knocked on the door.

No answer.

"Mr. De Wynter?"

No answer.

Meg tried the door. Unfortunately, it wasn't locked. "Mr. De Wynter?"

She pushed the door open, mentally crossing her fingers.

There was Matt, lying on the bed.

With a knife stuck in his chest.

Meg had to keep from panicking. This was a show. A play. It took everything in her to stay in character. "Someone call 911," she said, her voice only a little shaky.

"I'll do it, ma'am," Molly said.

Meg walked over to the bed, but then turned back. "Everyone out until the medics get here."

The guests scribbled, even as they backed out of the room.

Meg turned around to Matt and leaned down, checking his pulse. "You better be faking, buddy."

She couldn't believe how scared she was. Or

why. This was just getting a little too spooky. "Talk to me. Now."

"I can't. I'm dead."

She almost collapsed with relief. "You son of a—"

"It's not nice to speak ill of the dead."

"I'd kill you myself if I didn't dislike prison so much."

His lips quirked.

"What do we do now, brainiac?" she asked. "This wasn't part of the plan."

He cracked open one eye. "What part of the plan actually happened?"

Meg waved. "That's not important now. The problem is you just gave me an alibi. I can't be your killer."

"We'll work that out later," he said, then closed his eyes again as there was a knock on the door.

Meg snapped straight. "Come in! Hurry!"

A slew of people crammed into the room. "Is he...dead?" asked the actress playing Agatha Bond.

"As a doornail," Meg replied. "Are the police on the way?"

Molly sneezed. "Yes, ma'am."

"She doesn't seem terribly upset," Mr. Danks noted. Everyone scribbled.

Oh, right. She should be upset. And he needed to breathe. She hovered over him, crying, "Why? Why? Why?" and as people continued taking notes she whispered, "Breathe while you have a chance, dummy."

He took a breath and whispered, "Aren't you going to kiss me goodbye?"

"Not even if you were my lover, lover."

He started to grin, so she pinched him. Then she quickly straightened and turned.

Meg pulled the bell chain. The butler arrived a few moments later—his eyes a little glassy, his clothes a little disheveled. Uh-oh. He'd been hanging out with Glenda.

"Jeeves," she said. "Please escort all of our guests down to the library. I'm sure the police will want to interview everyone, so please, nobody try to leave the estate."

It took Jeeves a good two minutes to get all the rubberneckers herded out of the room. When they were finally gone, Meg stomped to the door and closed it, turning the lock with a vengeance. "Way to go, brainiac. We were all together when you commanded me to come upstairs. Now no one can be your killer."

He sat up on his elbows. "Oh. Well, what are you going to do?"

"Me?" she practically shrieked.

"Well, after all, you're the improviser in this crowd."

"I didn't improvise you getting knifed while the entire gang was in the library."

He waved. "You'll think of something."

She was thinking of something all right. Like finding a real knife to stick in his chest. "Since when did you embrace the idea of going with the flow, Mr. Listmaker?"

He shrugged. "When in Rome…" He wondered about that, too. Normally he'd be trying to get back on script, but somehow keeping Meg flustered was growing appealing.

"Let lions loose on you in the Colosseum."

"You really are a bloodthirsty wench."

Actually, even the sight of fake blood on his chest was making her stomach twist into knots. She plopped down on the bed, a little afraid her knees were going to give out on her.

"How about this?" she said. "How about if we plant a tape player in here that has your voice on it?"

He looked about as befuddled as she felt. "Why?"

"Well, the guests could infer that I taped your voice earlier, then somehow played it back in front of them to give myself an alibi."

He sat up. "You know, that could work."

"There's just one problem."

"Only one?"

"I don't have a tape player."

"Oh."

Meg tapped her lips. "Of course, the killer would be an idiot to leave a tape player in plain sight. Maybe I could sneak out tonight and get one, then hide it somewhere."

"There you go!" he said, then grabbed her face and planted a big one on her lips. "See, I knew you'd think of something."

Meg vaguely thought that she wouldn't have had to think of something if he'd stuck to the script, but she was just a little too occupied wishing they could spend a night, or maybe a year, kissing.

A KNOCK AT THE DOOR had Matt dropping down into his death pose.

He heard Meg make her way to the door, and sort of mourned that he had to keep his eyes closed so he couldn't also watch.

"Who is it?" Meg asked.

"Richard Tracy, Charleston PD," a man said.

Meg turned the dead bolt. "He's in here."

For what seemed like an interminable time, people filed back in and milled around making observations while the faux detective grilled Meg and she pretended to tell him all she knew. Matt took exception to a few of her adjectives. Like "obnoxious." Like "tyrannical." Like "a real horse's patoot."

"My goodness," one of the guests said. "Not a very nice way to describe a lover."

Matt's thoughts exactly.

Meg didn't try to save herself by singing his praises. She just kept ranting on to the fake detective about what a jerk he was. It was getting on his oxygen-deprived nerves.

And the guests scribbled on, as if he had all the time in the world not to breathe.

Finally Meg somewhat redeemed herself by saying, "Of course, I really loved him."

"She did it," somebody whispered.

"How? She was with us when he called down to her. And on the stairs."

Matt was only following this line of logic in a perfunctory way. He was a little busy allowing the sound of Meg's voice saying she loved him echo in his ears. It was an act. He knew that. He did. Really.

Then why had it sounded so good?

He was oxygen-deprived, that's why.

The actor playing the detective was apparently dictating his observations into a recorder.

"Victim appears to have a single knife wound to the chest. No sign of theft as yet."

He looked at Meg. "Who are you, ma'am?"

"Madeline Hatter, Mr. De Wynter's personal assistant."

"Are you the one who found the body, ma'am?"

"Yes."

"What time?"

"Around nine?"

"It was nine on the nose," said the cat-toting guest. "The clock in the library chimed right then."

As if they were invisible, which they were supposed to be, the faux detective ignored that. "And when you arrived up here, the man was dead?"

"As a doornail," Meg repeated. Then she once again remembered herself and let out a sob and a moan.

She glanced back at Matt, just in time to see a faint quirk on his lips.

"Has anything been touched?" Detective Tracy asked.

"She touched the body," one tattletale whispered loudly enough to be heard across the ocean.

"I went to check his pulse," Meg said.

"She's lying," another observed. "She leaned over and shook his body."

If Meg wasn't supposed to ignore them, she'd turn to them all and stick her tongue out at them.

"Well, go join the others in the library. I'll want to interview them all separately, but I want everyone together until the coroner and crime scene unit arrive."

Meg leaned over Matt one more time, caressed his cheek—which was a little stubbly, she realized—and gave him a chance to fill his lungs once again. "Goodbye, turkey."

She turned back and said, "I think everyone should be down in the library, don't you? You can come and report anything else you might find in here. Maybe that'll help you sort it out."

"Good idea."

It took a lot of body language before the paying guests got the hint that she meant all of them. She didn't want a real life corpse on her hand, even if he was an utterly infuriating live person.

11

IT WAS a very, very long four hours later before Meg could sneak Matt back into the house through the secret passage. Strangely enough, she'd been unusually happy to see him again, but decided to write it off as relief.

She led him through a maze that she'd explored several times to get the lay of the land. She'd discovered what almost looked like a sitting room directly behind the bookcase in the library.

Matt looked around thoughtfully, probably trying to discover the lever that would gain him entrance into the library proper, but if he was thinking it was in the bookcase, the man had no imagination.

Meg set the kerosene lantern on a rough wooden table beside an old-fashioned love seat, and the picnic basket Glenda had put together for them on a faded, but amazingly lovely, Persian rug.

His jaw dropped as he took it all in. "What, did this used to be an extra room?"

"If you ask me, it was always supposed to be a

hidden space. Maybe where those who knew about it held secret trysts."

He sniffed the air. "It's not musty or dusty or anything."

"There's ventilation and a dehumidifier."

"Was it like this when you got here?"

"No, I, umm, took the liberty of upgrading and having it cleaned. I don't do well with dust."

"Me, either!" he said, as if they'd just both simultaneously discovered they might be twins separated at birth. "Thank you."

She peered at him in the soft lamplight. "You're not angry?"

"Hell, no! I probably would have been choking and sneezing so badly they could have heard me in the next county." He hesitated, then in a lower voice said, "They can't hear us, can they?"

"Not unless we start screaming at each other." She gave him a menacing look. "Which, by your behavior tonight, is a distinct possibility."

He chuckled, and Meg hated how gorgeous he looked when he was amused. He wrapped his arm around her shoulders and hugged her. "Oh, my beautiful paramour, how could you scream at me when you're in such deep mourning at my untimely demise?"

She couldn't help it. Exhaustion, she decided, made her do it. She laid her head on his shoulder. "I could argue the untimely part."

His fingers began tracing her shoulder. Meg would protest if it didn't feel so darn good. "Meryl Streep you are not, Ms. Renshaw."

"Oh, and you're Lionel Barrymore? You practically began laughing."

"You'd have found a way to explain it."

She lifted her head and peered up at him. Exasperation gave way to wonder. "Since when have you turned into 'go-with-the-flow' guy?"

"Oh, don't worry, I'm not. But I have to admit it's been fun watching you. I've never met anyone quite like you, Meg."

She didn't know whether that was a compliment or not and wasn't about to ask.

Suddenly he cocked his head. "What's that noise?"

Meg leaned over and did something to a box on a side table, and the sound got a little louder. "It's Jeeves adding logs to the fire."

"What is that thing?"

"An intercom."

"You have the room bugged?"

"Temporarily!" She rushed to assure him. "We have to know when we can go in and out of the room undetected."

She pointed at a button underneath a small antique-looking mirror. "And if you push that you get a view of the room, too. The former owners must have visited some kind of spy store. I'm not sure what they were doing—maybe listening in on gossip or business deals?—but they had some nice tricks."

"Why?"

"Same reason. We want to see what people are doing." She laughed, a throaty sound. "But we can close it if any hanky-panky starts to happen. I'm not a voyeur as a rule."

Matt got stuck on hanky-panky for a second, but then moved right on to the voyeur part. Not that he was one, of course. But a mental image of installing a camera in Meg's shower popped into his head. Not that he'd ever entertain such an idea, but to deny the appeal of watching her suds herself up in all her naked glory was pretty futile.

To take his mind off the possibilities, Matt leaned closer to the mirror and said, "So, is the camera hidden behind an eye in a portrait, or something?"

"You watch too many old murder mysteries, Mr. Rossi. No imagination."

"Then where is it?"

"Remember the nude bust?"

Could she come up with more enticing words to fire his imagination? "Vaguely. The one in the corner?"

"That's the one."

"Oh" was the most intelligent thing he could think of to say. "Umm, wouldn't that be a place where people would…you know…look closely?"

"But most men would only concentrate on one area. And it's hidden pretty well."

Now that was a challenge. "Which one, the left or—"

Just then a loud sneeze sounded through the speaker. "Are you certain I can't get anything for you or...your cat, Mr. Danks, sir?"

"Who's that?" Matt whispered.

"Molly the Maid."

"No, thank you," a male voice answered. "We're just looking for clues."

"I'm not certain you're supposed to be pocketing the knickknacks, sir."

Meg shot forward and punched the button, and a grainy blank-and-white image of the room flickered on in the mirror.

"Evidence, miss," Mr. Danks said, holding a sterling silver candlestick in one hand and his humongous gray tabby in the other. "And I believe you shouldn't be following me around. I can't properly investigate."

"Mr. Klepto, in the library, with the candlestick," Matt whispered.

Meg laughed softly. Then they watched as Molly sneezingly excused herself with a disappointed look on her face, and Mr. Klepto continued to roam the room. They watched in awe as he then proceeded to pocket a Waterford crystal ashtray.

"Holy shi—"

"Uh-oh," Meg muttered, and stood up.

"Where are you going?" Matt said.

"Damage control."

MATT WATCHED MEG make her way back toward the secret side entrance at the west end of the house. In spite of the thieving jerk looting his library, he smiled. He couldn't help it. Even as she tried to trot in ugly gray heels, she looked luscious.

In fact, even in that godawful Miss Prim get-up, she looked sexy.

Which was ridiculous. But somehow appropriate. Most of the women he knew wouldn't be caught dead dressed down to look dowdy. It didn't seem to faze her in the least. To him that signaled a certain confidence in her own skin and attributes.

Meg Renshaw didn't feel the need to impress anyone. True, she was fanatical about succeeding at her job. But that was a plus. He was a fanatic, too.

And although Meg's view of how to accomplish her goals wasn't anything he could stand for any length of time, it occurred to him that for this weekend he was going to enjoy watching her in action.

And even though he'd love to see her in another kind of action, he was fairly positive that wasn't going to happen. The woman might be impetuous and spontaneous, but he had the feeling she was also very discriminating about whom she had a short fling with.

If she'd ever even had a short fling.

He wished he could just ask her. "So, Meg, how do you feel about a one- or two- or three-night stand? You know, just for kicks and mutual pleasure?"

He snorted in self-disgust. His mother would smack him upside the head. Although he'd bet Meg wouldn't. He'd bet she'd just laugh in delight and consider it a joke. Or pretend he meant it as a joke, just to save him the embarrassment of rejection.

Once she was out of sight, he sighed and turned back to the monitor to see what other little goodies the man would try to pilfer. He couldn't believe that anyone who could afford a weekend like this would stoop to theft.

Before the man could pocket anything else, Matt watched Meg fling open the doors, then stride into the room as if she fully expected it to be empty.

She stopped short, then glanced around, acting as though the guy wasn't even there. That's when Matt remembered she wasn't supposed to acknowledge the presence of the paying guests when she was in character. How was she supposed to confront him on his thievery if she couldn't even speak to him?

Knowing Meg, she'd find a way.

Tapping her forefinger on her chin, she went, "Hmm. Something seems wrong here. Whatever could it be?"

Matt watched in amusement as Mr. Danks kept jumping out of her way whenever she headed in his direction. She rearranged coffee-table books, then stood up straight. "It seems the Waterford ashtray is missing. Well, possibly Molly is cleaning it. I must ask her."

Matt snorted.

She then wandered to the fireplace. "Something is amiss here as well. It's…off balance somehow." She pondered, then her fists went to her hips. "One candlestick is missing. Molly wouldn't take one and not the other if she planned on polishing."

Too bad the picture was so grainy. Matt would have loved to see the sweat glistening on the pilferer's forehead.

"I would have considered this important information to pass on to the detective if it weren't for the fact that my darling Lionel was stabbed with one of his hunting knives."

Hmm, Matt believed she'd just passed a clue on to the man. He was pretty certain that no one had identified the murder weapon as having been from De Wynter's own collection of hunting knives.

While she continued to roam, Matt watched Mr. Danks slip the ashtray back onto a side table, and stealthily replace the candlestick on the floor beside the leather chair.

"Oh, there's the other candlestick," Meg said. "It must have fallen from the mantel."

With one more sweep of the room, her eyes lit on the ashtray. "And there! My goodness, I'm going to have to give Molly a good talking to about replacing things just so. She knows how particular Mr. De Wynter is." She paused dramatically. "Or should I say was," she said, then actually cackled with glee.

Now there was another clue. The woman gripping his dead body and sobbing up in the bedroom was now revealing that she wasn't exactly heartbroken at his demise.

For some strange reason, Matt felt a little insulted.

The man clutching the cat had eyes wide as saucers. He sidled toward the oak library doors.

Matt didn't know what got into him. He stood and banged on the wall, then flicked a switch and whispered in his best menacing Vincent Price impression, "You will pay for this! A-hahahahaha."

Obviously they'd both heard him, because they both jumped a little.

Cat-man stood frozen, eyes wide.

Even Meg appeared shaken for about a nanosecond. Then she relaxed and sighed. "Our ghost appears to have returned."

The man zoomed out of the room faster than a Formula One race car.

Meg glanced over her shoulder at him, then calmly strolled to the doors and shut them. Sashaying back into the room, she looked straight at the camera. She graced him with the most delightful smile he'd ever seen, then gave him two thumbs-up, winked and blew him a kiss. After which she turned to leave.

As he watched her sweet, sweet bottom sway, his heart gave a lurch. For some reason her happiness and approval meant more than it should. But it did.

And he found himself wondering just how she planned on rewarding him.

Matt couldn't wait to see what happened next.

12

MEG PRACTICALLY FLEW through the passageway back to Matt, feeling flushed with success. But when she arrived at the sitting area behind the library, he was nowhere in what little sight there was.

Disappointment brought her down. But that morphed quickly into worry. Where could he have gone? Was he all right? He was new to these back alleys, and could easily have wandered off and gotten lost. After all, he didn't have detailed floor plans to follow. And following detailed plans seemed to be the only thing he was any good at.

Well, he played a pretty mean ghost, she decided. And a somewhat believable dead guy. And he kissed all right, too. More than all right.

Meg shivered as she recalled the feel of his warm hands through the flimsy silk of her negligee. At the time she'd been a little too self-conscious, kissing a stranger in slinky attire in front of even more strangers.

But in hindsight, she was kind of sorry that she hadn't savored the moment more. And now that he was a corpse, they wouldn't be reenacting any scenes like that one again.

Damn.

She opened the drawer on the side table and pulled out one of several flashlights she'd stashed there days ago. Flicking it on, she looked left, then right, trying to decide where to start her search for the idiot. Since she hadn't passed him coming in, she turned in the opposite direction, heading toward the back of the house and the stairs that led up to the floors above.

Swinging her flashlight back and forth, she kept whispering, "Matt? Matt? Where'd you go?" all the while kicking herself for not telling him to stay put. It didn't bode well that she couldn't even keep track of her corpse.

Suddenly ahead of her she saw a disembodied flicker of light, seemingly bouncing down the steps ahead. "Matt?" she whispered again.

"Coming," she heard, and felt relief all out of proportion to the situation.

A few interminable seconds later his outline and then his face came into view. She'd be ready to ream him a new one if it weren't for the fact that he had a triumphant, boyish, I-just-caught-the-frog look on his face.

His smile was infectious. So when she said, "Where have you been?" it didn't hold an ounce of heat.

"Just doing my job, ma'am."

"Excuse me?"

"My spirit was restless. It felt the need to roam the house and give the guests a little piece of my mind."

Meg's jaw dropped, but then she chuckled. "You've been spooking the guests?"

"Indeed."

"If I'm not mistaken, Mr. Rossi, you just engaged in a little bit of spontaneous fun."

"Hey! I know how to have fun."

Meg decided not to point out that from what she'd heard, his idea of having fun was planning it step-by-step, way in advance. "Sure you do," she said, nodding as sincerely as she could.

Matt tapped her chin. "That was a fine piece of acting back there in the library, Ms. Hatter. You were an inspiration."

Meg felt a burst of pleasure. "Maybe there's hope for you, yet." The pleasure withered when she saw a flash of hurt flash in his dark eyes. "I'm just teasing," she said quickly. "Really, there's… lots of hope."

That was probably not the most brilliant thing to say. Matt looked down and gave a quick one-two shake of his head. When he looked up again, he was smiling, but it wasn't exactly a happy smile. "Nope, you're probably right. I'm pretty much hopeless in your eyes."

Meg wanted to stamp her foot, but that would

probably just look childish. "That's just not true," she said softly. "I never give up on people until they give me good reason to. And you just gave me a great reason not to."

She took his arm and turned back toward the library, noting not for the first time that the guy had some pretty impressive muscles under there. "Now tell me, who did you haunt?"

THEY BROKE OUT the goodies Glenda had packed for them. Turkey and ham sandwiches, a variety of chips, rum cookies that could fell an elephant, and— bless her lushy little heart—a bottle of cabernet.

While they sipped wine out of paper cups, they planned their next moves.

Although it was the middle of the night, Meg looked as fresh as if she'd just awoken from a great night's sleep. She'd taken off the wig, unbuttoned the prim collar of her shirt and rolled up the sleeves. Matt had asked why she didn't change out of that ugly gray skirt, but she'd just wrinkled her nose and said she had to be prepared to be Maddy Hatter at any given moment.

He, on the other hand, had changed into jeans and a polo shirt soon after the "coroner" had carted him out of the house. Thank goodness they hadn't tried to take him out in a body bag, but instead had just draped a sheet over his head.

"Are we doing any more haunting tonight?"

he asked, kind of hoping she'd say yes. He had to admit that it had been fun.

"Do you think it's necessary?" Meg asked after a dainty sip of wine.

Was she actually asking his advice? Or was she gently saying it was a harebrained suggestion? "It might not be necessary, but it could be fun."

An impish smile curved her lips and lit up her eyes. In the light from the lantern, they gleamed sea-foam gray. "Yes, it could."

Matt wrapped his itchy fingers around his cup to keep from reaching out and stroking her cheek. He probably would have done better to slap one of his hands over his mouth. "You know, you're really beautiful."

Unfortunately, his timing wasn't the best. She'd just taken another sip of wine. It splooshed out and sprayed his jeans and the lower part of his shirt.

She squealed in horror and grabbed for some napkins. "Oh, I'm sorry!" she said, beginning to dab at the wet spots. So mortified was she that she didn't even realize exactly where she was drying him off.

If she didn't cut it out—

He stilled her hand and gently took the napkins from her. "It's all right," he said, chuckling. "I don't blame you for being startled."

"I just…just…wasn't expecting that."

"No doubt."

Her smile was wobbly, but she finally said, "Remind me to light my entire apartment in lanterns."

MATT WOULD BE kicking himself over blurting out that comment to Meg and flustering her, but frankly he was having too much fun to worry about it right now. They stalked around the house, planting clues and freaking out the sleeping guests with strange noises and voices. Behind the bedroom of John and Lola Hopkins, they carried on a totally improvised slapstick between two bickering ghosts.

"Just because you're here now," Meg said in an eerie voice that would have Matt applauding if he could, "doesn't mean you have a ghost of a chance with me."

"You haven't seen what a specter I make without my sheets on."

"Mr. De Wynter, I will not have you scaring the guests in my home," Meg said. "That is my job."

"Ms. Foster, this house has not been yours for nearly a century. And may I say, you're well preserved for an old spook."

"Why, you…you…you…phantom. Don't let the wall hit you in the ass on your way out."

Matt nearly lost it. He slapped the back of his hand over his mouth to keep from breaking out in laughter. Meg stood looking at him with lips pressed together, her eyes bright enough to light up the entire passageway.

Finally Matt couldn't stand it, and flicked off the switch to the intercom. He dragged her down the passage and finally let loose with laughter. She joined in, and the sound of her giggles did something to him. He lost his mind, grabbed her and hugged her.

His first sensation, after the sound of her gasping in his ear, was the sense of how fragile she was. It wasn't that she was twig thin by a long shot, but her bones just felt so delicate beneath her blouse. It had been so long, he'd forgotten that women felt so good.

It suddenly occurred to him, too, that he could inhale her scent forever. "Ghosts aren't supposed to smell this nice."

"How are they supposed to smell?"

"I don't know. You're my first."

She laughed, but pulled away. "So now you know. We actually smell okay. Ghosts are people, too, you know. We shower with the best of them."

He stopped just short of blurting, "Want to shower with me?" Instead he said, "What next, boss?"

"Time to sleep."

"Are you sleepy?"

"No. But we probably should."

"Or we could raid the wine cellar and hang out behind the library to see if anyone shows up." He really hoped she felt like hanging out. He couldn't sleep if she knocked him out with a mallet. Oops. Better not suggest that.

She pondered, then smiled. "Sounds like a plan."

They headed down toward the entrance to the kitchen pantry, holding hands, which felt really good.

"Just out of curiosity, where am I supposed to sleep tonight?" Matt asked.

Meg stopped dead in her tracks and turned to him. "Didn't I tell you? With me."

"With…you?"

"In my room, dummy. You can't sleep in the crime room."

Matt had to work hard not to fall on his knees and give thanks. "Well, then, I'm sleepy."

"Want to raid the wine stash anyway?" she asked. "We could have a slumber party."

"Sleep is the furthest thing from my mind."

She chuckled. "You just said you were sleepy."

"Not when we can play truth or dare."

"Been to a lot of slumber parties, have you?"

"I've heard rumors."

She held up the lantern next to his face. "Are you going to be good?"

"Do you want the truth, or is that a dare?"

13

When had Meg lost her mind? Calm, cool, collected Meg, who handled anything thrown in her way. Except she hadn't planned on a roadblock named Matthew Rossi.

She liked him. Not that she didn't try to like most people, but it would be a whole lot less complicated if he were a bigger jerk all of the time instead of just on occasion.

And the fact that he showed up in her room dressed in gray sweats and a white T-shirt didn't help matters. He looked too comfortably shabby in a really sexy way. Maybe having him bunk on her couch hadn't been the best plan she'd concocted.

He was sprawled out on her couch, sipping the cabernet she'd swiped from the cellar. His five o'clock shadow gave him a dangerous air that she probably shouldn't be noticing.

Meg settled into a Queen Anne's chair and crossed her legs. She'd changed into sweats and a baggy T-shirt herself, but somehow she had the feeling they didn't quite make her look sexy the way they did him. Which was just as well.

Sort of.

She watched while Matt pulled out his pocket notebook and begin sifting through pages. "What now?" she asked.

"Truth or dare?"

"Excuse me?"

"Truth or dare. You promised we'd play."

"I was kidding."

"Well, I'm not."

"You actually made a list?"

He glanced up at her. "While you were getting the wine. Two of them. One for truths, one for dares."

Meg laughed. She couldn't help it. "You are some piece of work, Mr. Rossi."

MEGAN RENSHAW was a piece of work, too. Actually, a work of Mother Nature's artistry.

A week ago he would have said she wasn't his type. A week ago he'd have said he was drawn to professional, workaholic females who had all of their ducks in a row. Women who had game plans and stuck to them.

Well, that was still his type. Someone like his corporate attorney, JoAnn. Now that woman had a set slate of goals. She knew what she wanted, and she went after her ambitions with a vengeance.

So why hadn't he ever considered JoAnn as dating material? Their work relationship notwithstanding, JoAnn was perfect. She was as driven as he was. She'd expressed interest in starting a family someday. She was certainly pretty and smart.

Maybe he'd ask her out next time they met. Maybe he'd explore a more personal relationship.

Maybe he'd take the next alien spaceship to Mars.

"Earth to dead guy."

Matt blinked. "Huh?"

"I know I'm not exactly scintillating, but you're in another world, buddy."

"More like another planet."

"What?"

"Never mind. So, who goes first?"

Meg shook her head. He couldn't really blame her for being confused. He was confused, too. But he wasn't sure why. Which made it all that much more confusing.

She rubbed her temples with eyes closed. When she finally looked at him again, she smiled, although it looked kind of painful. "You've got the list. So go ahead."

"Truth or dare?"

"Truth."

He checked his notebook. "Do you have any siblings?"

Her mouth dropped open a little. "Are you serious?"

"Sure. What's wrong with that question?"

"You've never played this game before, have you?"

"No, but I still don't see anything wrong with the question."

She grinned, which would have irritated him if she didn't have such a beautiful smile. "I have three brothers and two sisters."

"Where are you in the ranks?"

"That's two questions."

"This was a multipart question."

"You've never played and you're already cheating."

"Sue me."

She chuckled. "I'm the oldest."

That shocked him. "Really?"

"Yes. Why do you look shocked?"

"Well, I always thought that the oldest kid had to take responsibility for the younger ones occasionally."

"Occasionally? How about all the time?"

"Really?"

"Absolutely. Both my parents worked. I was the built-in baby-sitter."

"But you're so...so..." He sputtered to a halt because he didn't know the right adjective to use that wouldn't come out sounding insulting.

"Irresponsible?"

"No! More like...spontaneous."

She laughed. "Are you an only child?"

"Yes."

She stopped laughing. "Oh." After a sip of wine she said, "Consider yourself lucky."

"I hated being an only child."

"Why?" she asked, tilting her head.

"It was…I don't know. Lonely, I guess."

She seemed to ponder that for a moment. "Isn't it funny? I would have given anything for lonely at times."

They sat quietly for a moment, then Matt said, "Okay, next question. Why aren't you—"

"Not a chance, pal. My turn. Truth or dare?"

Matt hesitated, because he almost wanted to hear what Meg would dare him to do. Then again, probably not. "Truth."

"Are you gay?"

Matt almost dropped his goblet. "What?"

"You heard me."

"Why would you think that?"

"You're gorgeous. You're rich. And you aren't married."

"You think I'm gorgeous?"

She rolled her eyes. "Oh, please, like you don't know it."

He somehow liked this line of questioning. "I'm glad you think so."

"Don't go getting cocky on me. Gorgeous doesn't necessarily equate to nice."

"You sound like you have experience in the matter."

Meg waved. "We're talking about you. Why haven't you been snagged before now?"

"I haven't met the right woman."

"Have a list of 'rights,' do you?"

"You could say that."

"Oh, please, share."

"Share what?"

"The right woman. I'd love to hear the list you've drawn up for her."

He was beginning to get offended. "You know, there's nothing wrong with knowing what you want."

"Of course not," she said, patting his thigh like he was a kindergartner. "A plan is a good thing. So what's your game plan?"

"Well, eventually I want to be married."

"Married's good. What kind of wife? I'm sure you have a list."

"If you think you've figured me out, tell me what you think would be on my list."

"She'd have to be pretty."

"To me, sure."

"What's pretty to you?"

The scary thing was the first thing that popped into his mind was "you." "I don't know. I just know it when I see her." You.

"Sexy?"

"Absolutely."

"What's sexy to you?"

Unfortunately, the first thing that popped into his mind again was "you." So he scrambled to remember the perfect woman he was planning on nabbing once he met her. "Well, you know, comfortable in her own skin."

"So confidence is sexy."

"Yes."

"It has nothing to do with bust size?"

He felt more than a little offended. "Do I come off to you as that superficial?"

"You're a man, right?"

"Your point being?" he asked, crossing his arms over his chest.

She grinned at him. "I thought it was pretty self-explanatory."

"I'm dense. Lay it out for me."

"I'm just teasing," she said, but her grin was still firmly in place.

"Are you a man-hater?"

Her jaw dropped open. "Of course not. Your species is good for one or two things."

"Such as?"

"I think I'll let you use your imagination."

"I have been since I met you."

Funny enough, Meg blushed. Matt hadn't been going for that effect, but he wasn't too unhappy about it, either. She was beautiful when she blushed. Well, she was beautiful regardless, but blushing, she was even more adorable.

He was working hard at thinking of something else that would make her blush more, but before he could come up with something she said, "What else?"

Matt blinked. "What?"

"What else are you looking for in a woman?"

"Why, are you thinking of applying?" he asked, only half joking.

Unfortunately, she found that really funny. It took a good minute or two for her to stop laughing. "Actually, just curious what a guy like you is searching for."

What was he searching for? For some reason he couldn't remember any longer. He knew he had a pretty lengthy list somewhere, but he couldn't manage to drum up a single item. But she already thought he was an idiot, so he dug for an answer. "I want her to want lots of kids."

"How many is 'lots'?"

"I hadn't really fixed on a number."

She nodded. "You've got that procreation thing going on, right?"

"Something wrong with that?"

"Not at all. Really."

"You don't want kids?" he asked, and for some reason was a little apprehensive about her answer.

She pondered that for a moment too long. "Not in the foreseeable future, no."

"What about marriage?"

Her nose wrinkled. "Almost been there, almost done that."

For some reason his gut clenched. "What does that mean?"

"It means I was engaged for a short period of time," she said, shrugging.

She seemed way too casual. "How short?"

"A few months."

"What happened, if you don't mind my asking?"

"I showed up for the wedding. He decided not to."

Was the guy out of his freaking mind? "I'm sorry."

"Oh, don't be. He did me a favor."

"How so?"

"If I'd have married him, I probably wouldn't have this career."

"You consider this a career?" he said, then wanted to bite his tongue in half, especially when she looked completely insulted. "I mean, it seems more like you're having fun."

"I am having fun. Does a career have to be painful?"

"No. I said that all wrong. I'm sorry."

The speed with which her sour expression

melted away was totally endearing. This was not a woman who held grudges. After all, she was practically giving her stinking ex-fiancé credit for improving her life. "I know it's none of my business, but why did he change his mind? Cold feet?"

"Warm sister."

Matt felt his jaw drop about a mile. "Excuse me?"

"He decided he liked my sister better."

"Please tell me you're kidding."

"Nope. It's the honest truth."

"How…how did your sister handle it?"

"Let's just say she inherited my veil."

Matt tried not to let his horror show. How could any sibling do that to her sister? Strangely enough, though, Meg didn't look all that devastated. "You don't seem to be all that devastated."

She sucked in her lower lip for a moment, but her clear gray eyes didn't turn watery or anything. "It wasn't a picnic that day. But I really think it was the best thing to happen to all of us in the long run."

"Do you…still speak to your sister?"

Meg looked at him like he was a loon. "Of course! She's my sister. And the mother of my two nephews."

Matt downed a good portion of wine. "I know this is rude to ask—"

"Probably. But go ahead."

"Doesn't it feel strange to be around the man, when both you and your sister...you know."

She grinned again. "No, I don't know. Spit it out, Rossi."

He felt his face heat up, but he trudged on regardless of the land mines before him. "You know. You both were with him."

She burst out laughing. "If you mean in the biblical sense, only my sister has had that pleasure."

"No way!"

"Way."

"You're serious."

Her twinkling eyes didn't look the least bit serious, but she nodded. "I was a purist back then."

"Have you fallen off the wagon?" he asked, knowing his voice held just a little too much hope. After all, his number one goal right now—which came as a huge shock even to himself—was to be with this woman. But the thought of being a woman's first lover was daunting. He couldn't stand the thought of hurting a female in any way. Especially not when making love with one.

"What do you think?" she asked.

"I'm pretty much hoping you took the plunge at some point."

"Yeah? How come?"

He had the feeling she was just this short of laughing at him. Unfortunately, he wanted to know too badly and he was willing to risk it. "To tell you the truth, virgins scare me a little."

"Too much pressure for you?"

"Something like that."

She patted his chest. "Relax, cowboy. I gave up on sainthood soon after I shredded my wedding dress."

"Oh. Good."

"Now why does this information matter to you, again?"

How to answer her without insulting or offending her? "Well, I really enjoyed that, umm, scene back in the master bedroom. How about you?"

"I wasn't real thrilled about having an audience."

"Look around. No audience in here!"

Her fists hit her hips. "Are you propositioning me, Mr. Rossi?"

"That depends on whether you'd slap me if I did."

"I'm the non-violent sort."

"In that case, I'm propositioning you. I dare you, in fact."

She laughed and blushed all at once. "I don't usually make love to a man I've known two days."

"I think you should cut me some slack. After all, I let you murder me earlier tonight."

She seemed to ponder it. "And I have to admit, you kiss real good."

"Why thank you, darlin'. Right back atcha."

"And I have to admit I've never had ghost sex before."

Hope eternal was blooming in his chest. "No woman should go without trying it just once."

"Just once? What are you, some kind of wimp?"

"Ha. Try and find out."

"On the other hand," she said, tapping her cheek, "I'd hate to appear cheap and easy."

Matt almost gave himself whiplash shaking his head. "You are richly sensual, and you've been playing hard to get for at least the last fifteen minutes."

"They usually collapse faster, hmm?"

"Five minutes tops."

"Well, I'm holding out for twenty, just to make you suffer a little."

"That's months in dog years, you know."

She laughed. "Suffer."

"Can I kiss you while I endure the torture?"

She sighed. "I suppose. Just no drooling, okay?"

14

EXIT STAGE LEFT (You didn't actually think they'd want another audience, did you? Oh, you did? Well, okay.)
   ENTER STAGE LEFT

15

THE BEDROOM Meg had commandeered was once occupied by the first mistress of the mansion. Rumor had it that she'd moved out of the master suite and into this wing of the house after almost three hours of wedded bliss.

The room was decorated in burgundy and gray with Victorian furniture, featuring a huge, raised canopy bed at its center.

Meg glanced at the bed nervously, having serious second thoughts. She could count on two fingers men she'd been intimately involved with, and both of those relationships had been going on for months before culminating in lovemaking.

This was insanity, pure and simple. She barely knew this man, wasn't even certain she liked him. It wasn't in her normal *mental* frame of mind to act on pure animal attraction.

Actually, since she wasn't certain she'd ever experienced pure animal attraction before, she wasn't certain about that, either.

The war inside her must have made an appearance on her face, because he suddenly studied her intently. "Second thoughts?"

Her laughter squeaked a little. "And third and fourth."

He reached out and stroked her cheek. "You know, sometimes thinking is highly overrated."

"Ha! This from a man who probably has lovemaking down to a science."

He looked truly insulted. "I do not."

Meg crossed her arms over her chest. "Like you don't have a checklist."

"No, I do not," he repeated, this time through gritted teeth.

Meg laughed softly and put a hand on his chest. "Now don't go getting offended. There's nothing wrong with being, umm, organized."

He didn't look much appeased. "When it comes to making love, I don't use a script."

Oh, how she wanted to find out for herself. She took a deep breath. Keeping her hand covering his steady, strong heartbeat, she said, "Well, if you did, how would it go?"

His frown disappeared. "Really?"

"Just give me a rundown."

He paused for a second, and Meg could practically see him pulling out his mental pad and paper. "Well, first I'd probably kiss you senseless."

Meg nodded solemmly, even though her

heart jumped a beat. "That's a good starting place for sure."

"I'd pick you up and carry you over to that bed."

She swallowed. "I'm heavier than I look."

"Not a problem, I'm stronger than I look."

She doubted that. He already looked like a football player. "Good," she said, her voice coming out a little hitched. "Because I'd hate for you to drop me."

"Not to worry, darlin'. I wouldn't dream of it."

She was beginning to enjoy this immensely. "And then?"

"I'll lay you down, and kiss you some more."

It didn't escape her notice that he'd switched from a hypothetical to a foregone conclusion. If she were a lady she'd protest. She didn't, which didn't say much about her character, but at the moment she was beyond caring. "And?"

"Then I'll take my good old time getting you naked."

"How much time?" she whispered.

"How about if I just show you?"

They were rapidly reaching the point of no return. Meg hesitated for at least a second and the anticipation swirling around him was palpable. "Put your money where your mouth is, Rossi."

THEY HAD AN AUDIENCE.

The realization came to Meg slowly, seeing as

she'd been lost in Matt's lips, his touch. He'd kissed her for what seemed like hours, but wasn't nearly long enough. Then true to his word he'd picked her up and laid her down on the king-size bed. When he let her get a word in edgewise, she'd murmured for him to turn off the lights.

He'd let out a husky laugh and grunted, "Not a chance. I want to see you."

Although a little shy at the thought, she'd been too busy enjoying the taste and scent of him to protest. And she loved the way his solid, warm body pressed into hers as he lay atop her on the soft mattress.

But feeling the presence of someone else dashed frigid-water reality on her. Reluctantly she broke the kiss. "We've got company," she whispered.

"Huh?" he asked, and she repeated herself.

Matt's eyes cleared and he shoved to his elbows, and twisted around one way, then the other. "Nope, nobody here."

Meg pushed at his chest and he finally rose to his knees. She scooted out from under him, the fine hairs on the back of her neck standing on end. "I feel eyes on me," she said, still whispering.

He half smiled. "Probably mine. I can't take my eyes off of you."

She shook her head. "You have gorgeous eyes. These are creepy, goose-bump eyes."

"My eyes are gorgeous?"

"Pay attention. There are creepy eyes on us."

Matt sighed, gave Meg's cheek a stroke and stood up. "If there is, I'll find the culprit."

Meg grabbed his arm, her stomach suddenly tied in knots. "Wait! What if the person has a weapon?"

Matt gently loosened her death grip and leaned over to kiss Meg hard on the lips. "It'll be nothing compared to the wrath of Rossi. This jerk just interrupted a very important moment in my life."

Meg tried to smile, but couldn't quite pull it off. Something eerie was going on in her bedroom,

She had a hard time letting him go. A shiver slithered slowly up her spine. "Be careful."

"Meg, honey, look around. There's no one here."

"Someone is watching us," she insisted.

"Then I'll find the creep," he said, but she wasn't all that pleased with the sparkle of humor in his eyes.

Nor did she appreciate his inspection of the room. While she readjusted her rumpled blouse he even had the nerve to look under the bed.

But she couldn't shake the feeling. She glanced at the portraits over the mantel on the fireplace. It was presumably of the original mistress of the house, if her period dress was any indication. Meg stared at it for a while, half expecting the woman's beady eyes to move. But no, the eyes stared straight ahead, unnervingly still and disapproving.

Maybe it was just Meg's imagination after all. But then she looked to her left at the dressing table underneath the curtained window. "Umm, Matt?"

"Hmm?" he said, from inside the massive bathroom.

"Come here, please."

He strolled out of the bathroom, his hair disheveled, his shirt untucked, looking as delicious as a double fudge sundae. But she was a little too spooked to appreciate it at the moment.

"Look," she said, pointing at the dressing table.

He glanced at it. "What about it?"

"Did you light that candle?"

He stopped short, then turned around and looked at her. "No. Did you?"

She shook her head slowly.

"Maybe the maid did before we got here."

Her head kept swinging back and forth. "I would have noticed. I specifically told everyone no lit candles in the bedrooms. I didn't want any accidental fires."

"Too bad you didn't ban fire from Glenda in the kitchen."

"Very funny. How did that candle get lit?"

"Spontaneous combustion?"

Meg rolled her eyes. "Please."

"Well, if you're trying to tell me it was a gho—"

Just then a breeze gusted through the window, billowing the sheers and making the candle stutter, before going out. Matt walked over to the dresser and pulled aside the sheers. "Uh, Meg?"

She dreaded his next words. "Yes?"

He stepped aside so she could see and Meg's heart stopped dead.

The window wasn't open.

MATT KNEW THERE HAD TO BE a logical explanation for all of this. Maybe it was a magic trick. Someone could light the candle remotely.

He picked it up and inspected it. The candleholder was ornate brass, but there weren't any wires connected to it. He pulled the long burgundy taper from it, but it appeared to be an ordinary candle.

He pulled the sheers back again and tugged at the window, but it was latched from the inside and wouldn't budge. Besides, even if someone had managed to reach in and light the candle manually, the room was situated in the west wing on the second floor, and there were no trees or balcony outside to help a person get near the window.

"If this was a magic trick, it was a good one," he muttered.

"The ghost," Meg said, her voice low.

"I don't believe in ghosts." But damned if he had a better explanation.

"You have a better explanation?"

"Not at the moment, but I'm sure there is one."

He turned back around to find her standing. Her body was stiff and her face pale. She didn't appear frightened out of her skull, but she certainly wasn't still steeped in passion, either.

Which pissed him off at one very nasty jokester.

Kissing her was a dream. He'd dare say every man's dream. Those soft lips of hers molded against his in a sexy way he didn't think he'd ever enjoyed so much. And when he pulled away to kiss her cheeks and nose and throat, she made soft gaspy sounds that drummed right through his limbs. All of them.

And she smelled so good and felt so good and damn she was beautiful.

Yet there was an innocence hiding under that brave and bold exterior, too. The first time his lips had traveled down to her collarbone and began to nip lightly on it, she exclaimed, "Oh!" as if no man had ever done that to her before. For a woman in her mid-to-late twenties, that seemed almost unbelievable. But he had a good gut instinct about this lady; she not only hadn't been around the block, he'd be surprised if she'd ever made it to the corner store.

A wave of tenderness blanketed him. At least that's what he thought it was. It was the same feeling he'd had when his parents had given him his first puppy one Christmas. They'd hoped to make him go outside and play. And it had worked then.

But he'd never wanted to ravish his puppy, and he most definitely wanted to ravish Megan Renshaw.

He strolled over to her and took her shoulders. She shivered under his touch, but he was pretty sure it wasn't a passionate quake beneath his fingertips. "You know it's just a joke from some sicko, right?"

"Sure, just a joke," she said, sounding about as convinced as a dental patient at the words "this won't hurt a bit."

"Do you have any actors who practice magic on the side?" he asked.

"I didn't see anything like that in any of their résumés. Besides, I just can't imagine how anyone could have done that trick."

"Someone's just trying to spook you, honey."

"There is no one staying in this wing of the house but me, Matt. And the only person—well, besides you, now—who knows which room is mine is Tina. And she couldn't and wouldn't pull it off."

"Is there a secret passageway into and out of this room?"

"Not that I've found. And the plans don't seem to indicate enough space between this room and the outer walls."

"Maybe there is one. Maybe someone snuck in here while we were…busy."

"You honestly think we wouldn't have noticed someone creeping around my room?"

"I doubt I would have," Matt said with a shrug. "I was so into you we could have had an earthquake and I wouldn't have noticed." And that was no line.

She blushed at that, which reminded him just how soft and pretty her skin was.

"That's nice of you to say," she said, ducking her head.

"I don't have a nice bone in my body." He squeezed her arms. "Do you want to go to my room?"

She hesitated, then shook her head. "I'm sure there's a perfectly good explanation. I'm not letting any spook scare me off."

He grinned and fake-knocked her jaw. "There you go, slugger. Now...where were we?"

"Well..." She glanced around once more, then threw herself into his surprised arms, hugging him. "Somewhere around here."

He lifted her up a few inches from the ground, loving her enthusiasm and the feel of her body pressed to his. "Not quite right here," he whispered into the side of her head.

But suddenly her body went stiff as an ironing board as she apparently spotted something over his shoulder.

"What?" he asked, lowering her to the ground.

Her gray eyes were huge as she looked up at him. "Did you happen to notice the portrait over the fireplace?"

"You mean the pinch-faced biddy who looked like she was sucking lemons?"

"That's the one."

"What about it?"

She stepped back from him and grabbed his shoulders. "Take a look at her now." With surprising strength she swiveled him around.

And there, above the mantel, where once hung a picture of one of the most unpleasant-looking women he'd ever seen, was a portrait of Meg.

16

"THERE'S a logical explanation for this," Matt said, but he didn't think Meg heard him. Her face was blank, and from shoulders to toes she was shaking like a leaf in a windstorm.

Matt grabbed her shoulders and marched her toward the door. She walked like a zombie, and he was really worried she was going into shock. He considered picking her up, but thought it better to keep her moving on her own.

In the hallway, he stopped and forced her to face him. "Meg, honey, I need you to pull it together, here. I know you're scared, but we've got to plan our next move."

She stared at him, then blinked. "I'm okay now."

No, she wasn't, but he nodded anyway. "Where do you want to go?"

She pointed weakly to two doors down on the right, and he took her hand and walked her slowly in that direction.

Turning on the lights, he saw that it was a salon

or parlor or library or whatever you called these things.

Matt took a quick look around and was glad to see not a portrait in sight. All of the paintings were of nature shots: the ocean, the forest, a blooming garden. So unless the waves started undulating, the wind began whistling through the trees, or the flowers began wilting, he was pretty sure they were safe.

He sat Meg down on the sofa or settee or whatever people called those things, then went straight to a decanter filled with amber liquid. Whether it was Scotch or cognac, he didn't much care.

Splashing the liquid into two crystal snifters, he said, "This should help a little." He carried them back to her, setting one down and taking the other, wrapping her palm around it. She still shook, so he kept his hands over hers as he brought the glass to her lips.

Meg dutifully sipped slowly, and in a couple of moments the shaking in her hands began to subside. When he felt she could handle it, he released her hand and took a healthy sip of his own.

Then he stood and walked around the entire room, yanking candles from their holders. When he thought he had them all, he opened a drawer in a dainty mahogany desk and stuffed them inside.

Then he returned and sat, taking another pull of the cognac that burned all the way to his gut. Glancing at her, he was glad to see color returning to her cheeks. For a while there she looked like she'd seen a—

"What happened back there, Matt?" she asked, her voice still a little wobbly.

"Something perfectly logical, I'm sure. A magic trick or something like that."

Meg shook her head. "I don't see how."

"Well, we'll figure it out before this weekend's over."

"What if it really was…was—"

"It wasn't."

"But the legend…"

"Hogwash."

Setting down her snifter, Meg said softly, "Thank you for being there. I don't know what I would have done if you hadn't been here."

He shuddered at the thought, too. Not that he was a superhero or anything, but he hated the thought of Meg experiencing that weirdness alone. "So where do you want to go? My room?"

"No. Although the room is supposedly cordoned off, that probably won't stop nosy people from trying to break in for more clues."

"Then where?"

He could see the wheels chugging in that pretty head of hers, and thought that was an excellent sign. Meg was back.

After a moment she brightened. "How about the cottage on the east end of the estate? It's isolated, so we wouldn't be near any of the guests staying in the other guest cottages. I think it's the mother-in-law cottage."

A mother-in-law cottage. If any place would be haunted, that would be it. He didn't think he ought to say that, though. "Sounds like a plan. Is there room for two?"

"I'm sure there is."

"That's good, because there isn't a chance in hell I'm leaving you alone tonight."

"Thank you, Matt," she said so seriously, it nearly broke his heart.

"Hey, I like the company."

That thought sort of brought him up short. Normally, he hated company. He liked being alone after eighteen-hour days of meetings and phone calls and more meetings. But with Meg he looked forward to spending as much time with her as they had. Which felt kind of important and serious.

Not like he'd begun thinking about anything serious with her, anyway. Not really. Not that he was aware of, at any rate. This was just two ships passing in the night, pausing long enough to pleasantly dock.

Somehow he didn't think she'd appreciate the analogy.

He forced a smile and grabbed her hand. "Then let's get to it."

At the door to her room, Meg paused, squared

her shoulders and marched right in, avoiding looking at the portrait.

As she pulled what looked like shorts and a baggy T-shirt from her luggage, and a toilet kit from the bathroom, Matt could swear he heard her muttering, like a mantra, "You don't scare me. You don't scare me. You do not scare me."

Matt decided that another crystal decanter might be in order, so he picked it up from a side table. Meg finished gathering a small amount of stuff, then practically sprinted to the door, although he could tell she was attempting to do it with dignity.

Before he followed, Matt confronted the portrait head-on.

Staring back at him with an imperious glare and puckered face was the old biddy.

As THEY MADE THEIR WAY UP the winding staircase toward the east wing and Matt's room, Meg voiced the question she'd been dreading, but couldn't help but ask. "Did you look?"

"I did."

"And?"

"The bat's back."

She stopped dead in the center circular balcony. "She is?"

"Yep."

"Maybe we've been going about this all wrong.

Maybe we've been assuming the ghost is her murdered husband. Maybe she's the ghost."

"Meg, honey, there are no such things as ghosts."

"So you say."

"Well, before we're done here we'll have a totally logical explanation."

She glanced at him skeptically, but just nodded. "If you say so."

"I do," he said, less certain than he sounded. But he was so happy to see the color had returned to her cheeks, he wasn't going to try to start mulling it over out loud just yet. He'd think about it privately until an explanation came to him that would satisfy her. "Let's go before someone sees us."

"It's four in the mor—"

"Achoo!"

Meg glanced over the balcony to see Molly the Maid tiptoeing from the direction of Mr. Danks's bedroom. She growled. "Molly's on the prowl again with one of the paying guests."

"That's bad?"

"That's bad. Go get what you need and I'll meet you in your bedroom and we'll head out the east passageway."

"What are you going to do?"

"Kick some chambermaid butt."

THEY FINALLY HEADED for the east end cabin at around four-thirty in the morning. Meg was physically and emotionally exhausted, and was a little bit irritated that Matt looked fit enough to run a marathon.

Not to mention, he was touching her at every opportunity. A hand to her back here, fingers to her arms, wrists, cheeks, seemingly everywhere.

Not inappropriately, she had to admit. In fact, if she wanted to be honest, it felt wonderful. You could call the man a stick-in-the-mud, but he was a thoughtful, gentlemanly one.

She wasn't old-fashioned by any stretch, but to her way of thinking there was nothing more flattering than a man who showed courtesy.

Lord knew she'd drummed manners and common courtesy into her little brothers. They'd really resented her at the time, but they'd grown up to be fine men who women flocked to.

She remembered one time when her brother Justin was so eager to race into a toy store, he nearly knocked an older woman down.

For his trouble Justin received no toy that day, but instead garbage duty for a month. Justin hated her for a long time after that, but he sure as heck never made that mistake again.

Matt reminded her of her brothers in that way, and a wave of nostalgia almost knocked her over. As much as she traveled, she didn't get to see her siblings nearly as much as she'd like. But she took pride in learning from talking with their respective mates that they all treated their spouses right.

Matt would treat his wife right. He might drive her up a freaking wall with all of his organizing and planning and by-the-book mentality, but he'd still treat his wife right.

She definitely wanted her eventual mate to treat her with consideration and respect. She'd settle for nothing less.

She wanted her husband to be drop-dead handsome like Matt, too. It wasn't a top priority, but it sure would be nice to melt inside at just the kind of smoldering look Matt was shooting at her right now.

Meg nearly stumbled at the thought, and Matt was right there to keep her from landing on her back end.

"Are you all right?" he asked, sounding genuinely concerned.

No, I am not all right. I am comparing my future husband to you, you turkey. Stop setting impossible standards right this second. "Fine. I'm just…tired."

"I'm sure you are. And it's a big day tomorrow."

Matt stepped forward and unlatched the door, swinging it open. Meg began to walk in, but he flung a hand in front of her tummy. "Gentlemen before ladies."

Okay, she was getting gooier by the moment. To counteract that she said, "Where are we going to find a gentleman at this time of night?"

"You're not, so you'll have to settle for me."

Settling for him wouldn't be a problem, except she was too exhausted to try.

He found the lights after a little groping and flicked them on. He scanned the place for a couple of seconds, then stepped back, waving her through.

The first thing that hit Meg was the pine soap. No doubt, it wasn't the Ritz, but it was clean.

The cabin was almost beautiful in its quaintness. The front room was filled with old Shaker furniture, covered in a variety of colorful quilts. The fireplace was massive for such a small space, and, thank goodness, not a portrait in the place.

There was only one bedroom and Meg bit her lip.

Matt looked over at her then chuckled softly. He dropped his clothes on an old stuffed chair and the decanter on the coffee table. "I'll take the couch."

She looked at the couch then back at him. It was a large couch but he was a larger man by a foot. "No, no, you take the bed. I can fit on the couch, you can't."

"No arguing, sweetheart. Go get comfortable and then I'll tuck you in."

Meg opened her mouth but he gave her one shake of his head. "No. Go get ready for bed. I can't wait to see you in those sexy pj's you brought along. Then I'll tell you a bedtime story."

TEN MINUTES LATER Meg had changed into her shorts and the T-shirt, brushed all things that needed brushing and scrubbed all things that needed scrubbing. Matt had done the same, only his pajamas were sweats and sweats only, slung low.

Meg sucked in a breath at the first sight of his naked chest. A light sprinkling of hair ran a trail down its center, bisecting it into two equally breath-stealing halves. There wasn't an ounce of extra flesh on the man that shouldn't be praising glory it didn't belong to him.

She tried not to gape. She tried to look anywhere else. But that led her gaze lower, and all her sleep-deprived and possibly halfway insane brain could register was what he'd look like if those sweats suddenly took a nosedive to his ankles. She was literally speechless for the first time she ever remembered.

While she'd been gone, he'd scrounged what looked like a juice glass from the tiny kitchen and had poured a fingerful of cognac into it. "Not exactly crystal," he said, holding up the glass. "But you do what you can."

"Matt, if you want to share the—"

"Nope, not tonight. I don't take advantage of comatose women, and if I slept in there I'm afraid I'd break my own rule."

Relief warred with a boatload of disappointment. "Okay."

He took her arm. "Let's get you to bed."

Not since she was a tiny child had anyone

tucked her into bed. She'd always done the tucking. She'd feel a little foolish if she wasn't so happy about it.

He led her to the bedroom, where he must have pulled back the sheets on the queen-size bed while she'd been in the bathroom. Meg almost cried at the thoughtfulness of it all.

"Climb in, sweetheart."

She did, and he pulled the covers up to her chin. "Would you like a sip before bedtime?" he asked, and she shook her head. The bed could have been made of sheetrock, but it felt like a cloud to her right now.

Matt took a drink of the cognac, then set the glass down on the night table and settled down on the edge of her bed. "It's been a long night."

"Mmm-hmm. Longer day tomorrow," she murmured.

"We'll get through it together."

That sounded so good, but she was too tired to figure out why. "'Night, Matt, and thank you."

"Not quite, Meg. Give me your arm."

Confusion fogged her brain, but she did it automatically.

Matt laid it, palm up, across his thigh. Then he did the most delicious thing she'd ever experienced. He began stroking gentle fingers up and down the tender inner skin of her forearm and higher.

Meg sighed in utter bliss. This was heaven. "What are you doing?"

"When I was a little boy, and I didn't feel well, or if I'd had a rotten day, my mother would stick me in bed and give me what she called—and excuse the sissy name—arm tickles. No matter how sick or how upset I was, it just felt so good that it made everything bad go away."

"I love your mother," she mumbled.

"She'd love you."

Meg smiled, even as she felt herself falling into a void of peaceful contentment, and the delicious, gentle touch on her arm. "Anyone ever tell you that you're a charmer, Mr. Rossi?"

"Not a single person in the entire world."

"Dumb world."

"I've always thought so."

"Put it on your list."

"I'll do that. Ready for your bedtime story?"

"Yes, please. But don't stop the arm tickles."

"I'll have you know I can chew gum and walk at the same time, too."

She thought she smiled, but it just might have been on the inside.

"Once upon a time there was this beautiful...fairy."

"Fairy?"

"Yep, fairy. She flitted around and tried to help everyone, but somehow something always went wrong. But that never stopped her from trying."

"Well, she had to go with the flow."

"Indeed. Very exasperating fairy, she was."

She ignored that because she was too tired to fight. "Did she have a wand?"

"No, this one carried a water pistol."

This time Meg did laugh. "Smart fairy."

"Well, anyway, along came this ant."

Meg felt her eyebrows screw up. "Ant?"

"Yep, a fire ant. Very organized, very industrious."

"Oh. Those kind. They sting."

"Only if they're mad. Anyway, this ant thought the fairy was about the most beautiful creature he'd ever seen. In fact, he was surprised to discover that the fairy looked even more desirable in ratty shorts and a baggy T-shirt than she was in that flowing gown she usually wore at night."

Meg knew there was a metaphor in here somewhere, but she was giving up the good fight. Only snippets were penetrating, and darkness was winning control of her brain.

The last thing she thought she heard was something about "fire," "water" and "sting."

And the last thing she felt was a featherlight kiss on her lips.

17

When Meg woke up, Matt was gone and instead Tina, her assistant, was sitting on the couch, agitation beaming off her body like a spotlight.

Dealing with Tina before coffee was like playing a 33 album at 78 speed.

"We have major problems, boss."

"Another broken nail?"

"Not that bad. But bad."

"What's that?"

"Mr. Rossi's gone."

Meg came to full alert, as if she'd just downed three straight lattes. She tried to keep her voice calm. "Did he say why?"

"A glitch in a contract or something. He had to head into Charleston to meet with someone named Tracy."

"Tracy. Right." A woman. Not that there was anything wrong with that. "Did he say if he's coming back?"

"He said he'd try, but possibly not until tomorrow."

An all-nighter with Tracy. Terrific. Meg felt a headache coming on. Her brain whirled with all kinds of possibilities she really had no right to consider.

Matt's life was his own. He'd only been doing all of this as a favor to her anyway. He'd probably grown bored with the silliness of the entire idea when he had millions of dollars to play with and hundreds of properties to buy and sell.

Still, she couldn't help being irritated. He didn't seem the type to run out on his obligations. Then again, he wasn't really obligated, was he?

She ignored the gaping void that was digging its way through her stomach. And higher.

"Is there coffee?" she asked, searching for an excuse to buy time to think and calm down.

"In the kitchen. Matt sent me over with a pot, and some croissants, because Glenda wasn't done spiking the pancakes before he had to leave."

Meg headed straight for the kitchen, Tina hot on her heels. "What are we going to do, Meg?"

"Coffee first," Meg said, and it was probably the most terse statement she'd ever uttered to Tina.

Tina must have noticed, because she didn't press the point for once. "By the way, Matt gave me your Miss Hatter costume to bring to you."

"Wasn't that thoughtful?" Meg said, then pressed her lips together at the sarcasm in her voice. It wasn't like her to act like a shrew, just because someone disappointed her. She had no right. She knew that.

Coffee. She needed coffee.

Wasn't he the same guy that stroked her to sleep last night? And told her a fairy tale? He was probably just amusing himself since he had nothing better to do while he watched over his property to make sure they didn't trash it.

Tracy. Meg never did like that name.

After glugging down two cups of coffee, Meg finally faced Tina. "Okay, so what's the big deal?"

"Our dead man is gone!"

"Tina, let's think about it. The operative word here is…gone." She almost choked on that last one. "What do we need him for? No one expects to see him again." Including me. "In fact, it's probably easier. That way I don't have to be sneaking him around to keep the guests from running into him." And he won't be here to protect me from ghosts. "He was…a pain, anyway, with all of those plans and diagrams and lists. It's better this way."

Tina relaxed. "Maybe you're right."

Meg dragged a smile to her lips. "Of course I am." Jeez, I'm going to hell.

Tina actually conjured a smile. "Before he left, Mr. Rossi made certain to give all of the guests a wake-up spook."

Meg wasn't all that certain it was Mr. Rossi

doing the spooking. "Well, I guess he went out with a bang." She almost choked on that one.

"He said he'd try to get back. Do you think he will?"

"I don't know Mr. Rossi that well, but from what I've seen, if something's gone wrong with one of his projects, it'll drive him crazy. He'll stay wherever he is until the emergency is fixed." Or until we're gone.

Meg racked her brain, trying to figure out if she'd done or said anything to drive him away. Probably many somethings, which was a thoroughly depressing thought.

"So what's our next move?"

Meg rubbed her temples. "We have a lot to get done today. We'll need to time some of this stuff differently because of everything that...umm... changed yesterday. Let me get a pen and paper and let's make a list."

MATT STRODE ANGRILY into Tracy Weathers's office and without preamble said, "This better be good, Tracy, to interrupt my vacation."

Tracy's blue eyes widened. "I'm sorry, Matt, but you know I wouldn't have called if it weren't."

Matt ran a hand through his hair, which probably looked like hell. "I'm sorry, you're right." He stuck out his hand. "So how's Denise?"

Tracy shrugged. "Wives. Can't live with them, can't afford the alimony."

Matt laughed. "You old dog. If that gorgeous woman ever left you you'd be a drooling mess in a week."

Tracy winked. "If you think I'd admit that verbally, you've lost what young marbles you have."

Enough chitchat. Matt wildly respected this man, enjoyed his company, and certainly had benefited from his business acumen over the years. But Matt wasn't in the mood for business at the moment. Not when the only image in his mind was that of a softly sleeping goddess, who made sweet whimpering noises in her sleep whenever he stroked his fingers up and down her arm.

He'd sat with Meg long after she'd fallen fast asleep. He hadn't been able to help it. He couldn't seem to pull away from her side.

He'd ached to crawl in beside her and take her in his arms this morning, but his mother would bop him over the head if he ever did anything that smacked of taking advantage of a vulnerable woman.

He shook his head. "Is it the Dragon deal?" he asked.

Tracy tossed down a thickly bound sheaf of papers. "Yes. Legal has found a few clauses in the contract that rang some bells. We need to meet with them and hammer out a counter."

Matt's tie felt like it was strangling him for some reason. Was it less than a week ago that he'd have felt naked without a tie choking his neck? "So meet with them. You don't need me."

Tracy stared at Matt as if he'd just donated all of his assets to Bill Gates's retirement fund. "Of course we need you. We need to map out a plan."

"You know how to read maps."

"Only after you've charted them, my boy."

Suddenly the lack of sleep the last couple of nights weighed down on Matt. He felt immensely exhausted at the thought of sitting in boring meetings all day long, holding hands and planning, planning, planning.

He didn't know what was wrong with him, and wouldn't analyze it until the drive home. Back to the mansion, that was.

He lived for this stuff. It was his adrenaline rush. The art of the deal. The crafting, the step-by-step movement toward success. But right now, he was too tired. And he had another obligation that was more important to him right now than the 3.5 million he stood to make when this deal was signed and executed.

"Between you and Legal, you're more than capable of handling this." He stuffed the contract in his briefcase. "I'll look this over first chance I get, then go over the changes you think we need to make. I'll get back to you when I can."

Tracy was a big man, but Matt bet he could have knocked him over with a feather right about now. "Look, I'm on my first vacation in I don't know how long, and I don't want to stay here all day dealing with this. You guys don't need me right now."

"What's so all-fired important, Matt?"

"Taking time off."

"To do what?"

"Play dead."

DAY TWO of the murder mystery weekend was as much a disaster, if not more so, than day one. Meg and Tina spent the morning trying to get the actors into their respective places doing nefarious things that the guests would happen upon. Sherrie and Watson Holmes were supposed to be in De Wynter's study, attempting to break into his files, at 11:00 a.m. sharp, and work it for half an hour. They accomplished that just fine, but all of the amateur sleuths seemed to think that the key clue to tracking down the killer lay in the library instead, which wouldn't be seeing action until early afternoon.

Meg and Molly were supposed to be moving among the guests, giving hints as to where they should direct their attentions, but Molly had come down with a blinding migraine, no doubt due to cat dander overload.

So Meg had had to recruit Jeeves to take Molly's place. And of course Jeeves didn't know the meaning of the words "go with the flow."

As the guest couples hovered about, Meg told Jeeves, "Mr. Jeeves, I do not want the maid cleaning Mr. De Wynter's study until I've had time to put his papers in order. Understand?"

"Yes, ma'am."

Not the right response.

Meg tried again. "I certainly hope you haven't seen any of our guests in there since the murder?"

"No, ma'am."

Meg almost groaned. "Not even Sherrie and Watson Holmes? I believe I remember seeing them heading in that direction."

"Very possibly, ma'am. I was helping Mr. and Mrs. Bond down in the wine cellar, choosing tonight's libation."

"I see." If this were real life, she'd seriously consider firing good ol' Jeeves. The Bonds weren't due to be caught in the wine cellar until late afternoon.

Not to mention, none of the amateur detectives had stumbled upon the tape recorder she'd planted in Miss Hatter's room, even though the fake inspector had let it slip to all the guests at breakfast that he insisted on searching her quarters.

This was a whodunit all right. Not a person in the mansion—including Meg—knew who that who was.

Right before lunch, Meg stalked toward the dining room, cursing one Matthew Rossi. List-making, ha! What a waste of time. She'd have had more fun soaking in a nice hot bubble bath. And with about the same results.

Meticulous planning might work for anal types like Matt, but it certainly wasn't doing her any good. As she scowled down on her bullet-point notes. Not one had been crossed off as accomplished.

She tore the sheet from her clipboard as she entered the dining area, making certain to don her prude persona. "Good afternoon, ladies and gentlemen." She addressed the actors. "I trust you had a pleasant morning?"

"Pleasant?" Mrs. Drew replied in a near shriek. "I'll have you know that the maid has yet to make our bed, and has failed to deliver fresh bath towels. The ones in my bathroom are...soiled, and I must have them taken away at once."

Hallelujah. Someone who delivered her line correctly. The towels planted in her bedroom had specks of fake blood on them. Meg wanted to kiss the woman.

But as she checked the other table to see if anyone was jotting this down, she noticed they were more interested in the freshly baked rolls on the table.

"I apologize, Mrs. Drew. Our chambermaid has taken ill, so our usually impeccable accommodations are running a bit behind schedule."

"I won't have it. I want those towels out of there."

"Pass the butter, please," one of the guests said.

Meg wanted to bonk the guy over the head. "Is there a reason you want to be rid of the towels?" she asked, practically looking directly at the guests to give them a clue.

"Is there any strawberry jelly? I'm allergic to grape."

Meg refrained from rolling her eyes. Crumbling the useless list in her hand, she stalked over to the fireplace and tossed it in.

"Look! She's burning a piece of paper! I bet that's a clue."

If Meg weren't made of sturdier stuff, she'd have fallen on the floor and burst into hysterical laughter. An act of innocent defiance against all things Rossi, and now they see a clue.

Watson Holmes, bless his pea-pickin' heart, went with it. "What was on that paper you just burned, Miss Hatter?"

Meg turned with a jerk. She could ham it up with the best of them. "Why, I don't know what you mean."

"I saw it, too!" chimed in Agatha Bond, standing dramatically. "I believe you just burned evidence."

Meg fluttered her hand at her chest. "Oh, no, no of course not. That was…just a copy of yesterday's agenda for Mr. De Wynter."

"Did that agenda include taking one straight in the heart?" asked Detective Richard Tracy from the doorway.

"Oh! Detective, you startled me," Meg said. Then she squared her shoulders. "It was an innocent list. Nothing else."

"Well, we'll never know now, will we?"

"She's guilty as sin," one of the guests whispered.

"No, Detective, I don't suppose you will. You will just have to take my word for it."

"Now this is getting good."

"Pass the rolls, please."

"I suggest you don't make any plans to leave the premises, Miss Hatter," the detective said.

"I have no inten—"

"I know you did it," a menacing, disembodied voice said.

Matt.

"Did you hear that?"

"I heard it. That's the voice we heard last night and again this morning!"

"That's Mr. De Wynter's voice!"

All of the actors went stiff on cue, but none said a word.

"Did you hear that?" the detective asked, directing the question toward the actors' table.

"I didn't hear anything," Chancy Drew said with a nervous laugh.

"Nor I."

"Not I."

"Hear...umm...what?"

"Miss Hatter, did you hear it?" the detective asked.

"I believe I hear Jeeves approaching with the first course," Meg said. "I hope you all enjoy your meal. Detective Tracy, you are welcome to join our guests. But I have things to attend."

With that, Meg hightailed it toward the door, ignoring the detective's call to come back. As soon as she rounded the corner, she broke into a run, waving breezily at Jeeves as she passed him, pushing a cart filled with salads.

She ran down the hall and turned right into the library. Making certain no eyes followed her, she quickly entered the passageway and turned right again.

Realizing it was undignified to go running into his arms, she forced herself to slow to a walk, tried to force her racing heart to settle down.

She came upon Matt, just as he intoned, "You know who you are," for the benefit of the guests. But when he glanced over and saw her coming, he flipped off the sound and turned to her, a heart-melting smile on his face. "Why, Miss Hatter, fancy meeting you here."

She stopped short of flinging herself into his arms. Slapping a cool expression on her face, she said, "So, you decided to come back."

His smile faded. "Of course I came back."

"I wasn't sure you would."

"Why not?"

"Well, you left rather abruptly." She took a breath to try and erase the petulance from her tone. "Without leaving a note."

"I left a message. With Tina. Didn't she give it to you?"

Okay, she was acting like an immature brat. "Yes, she did. Thank you for that. Otherwise I would have worried that something nefarious really did happen to you."

"I would have woken you up, darlin', but you were sleeping so peacefully I didn't have the heart."

She would have rather he'd awakened her, but she couldn't be mad at him for trying to be considerate. He just better never do it again. "Well, how'd your meeting go?"

"It was a waste of a trip, but Tracy sounded desperate on the phone."

"Oh. Tracy."

He searched her face for a moment, looking puzzled. "Right. Tracy Weathers, one of my business partners."

"Oh. Well, I'm sure she's glad you went."

"She, who?"

Meg waved. "Tracy, dummy."

He stared at her for a moment before chuckling. Stroking her cheek, he said, "I think Tracy might take a little offense at you trying to put him in a dress."

"Tracy's a man?" she said, trying not to lean into his hand.

"That's what he says."

"Oh."

"You weren't jealous, were you?"

She conjured a scoff. "Of course not. Why would I be?"

"Oh, I don't know, maybe because I've become your favorite corpse?"

"Don't get too full of yourself, Rossi. You're my only corpse."

"Oh, good, I'm one of a kind."

Now there was an understatement.

"So what's next, boss?" he asked.

For some reason that warmed Meg, because she'd bet her right arm he hadn't called anyone boss in a long, long time. "We have to try and find us a killer."

"Who is it this minute?"

"Heck if I know."

He laughed. "All the more fun."

"It's going to be a long day, I'm afraid."

"Well, if you don't need me for a while, mind if I go back to the cottage and grab some shut-eye?"

She'd forgotten he was running on fumes. "Oh, of course not! I'll have Glenda send some lunch over, too."

"Thank you."

"And use the bed, all right? That couch is too small."

He shot her a smoky smile that made her tummy flip. "Thank you, I think I will."

"Good."

He scorched her with a kiss that would make a lesser woman swoon. Meg wrapped her arms around his neck and kissed him back as if he'd just returned from a year's stint overseas.

When they finally broke apart, Matt said, "Lady, you are all woman." He took what sounded like a steadying breath. "I think I'll go climb into bed for a while."

"Do that."

"And with any luck, I'll be climbing back in again tonight."

Meg could have pretended she didn't understand, but why bother? "Mr. Ghost, I have the feeling tonight's your lucky night."

18

THE AFTERNOON didn't fare much better, with one major exception. At two Meg snuck away and headed to the cottage, a picnic basket full of goodies in hand.

But when she arrived, he was so dead to the world she wouldn't have tried to wake him for anything.

He'd dropped off in boxer shorts, but apparently was a kicker, because the sheets and blankets were all bunched at the end of the bed, and he was sprawled on his back with arms spread wide.

Meg felt guilty ogling a vulnerable, sleeping man, but not guilty enough to stop. He was, simply—or sinfully—gorgeous. And if all went well, that body would be all hers sometime tonight.

Which sort of brought her up short because she wasn't quite certain when she'd made up her mind to go for the brass ring. This wasn't like her at all. But at this point, she didn't much care. She'd much rather be something of a hussy than to wonder for the rest of her life what it would be like to be made love to by this man.

She didn't know how long she stood there, staring at him, but finally she tiptoed out of the bedroom, regret that she couldn't just climb into bed beside him knotting her tummy. Unfortunately she had obligations, and one of them wasn't jumping into the sack with a man she barely knew.

While she searched for some way to leave Matt a note, she thought about the "barely knew" portion of that notion. True, she'd only known Matt for a few days, but it seemed like much longer than that. In fact, she had a hard time thinking back on the time when she'd had no idea that Matthew Rossi existed. And she also realized that for a certainty she'd never forget him as long as she lived.

She also realized that anything that happened between them would be temporary. She was sort of sad about that, but she was also realistic. They weren't meant to be anything long term.

He was ready to settle down and get married. To start a family.

Meg wasn't certain she even wanted children. Ever. She'd raised kids since she was a kid herself. She'd done her duty, and now it was Meg time.

Boy, that sounded selfish even to her own brain. But she wasn't going to lie to herself or to any man in her life. She just couldn't see herself as a mother all over again.

"Hello, sweetheart."

Meg jumped about a mile, then whirled to face a very rumpled and sexy Matt. "Oh, you scared me to death."

His smile was slow and sleepy. "Sorry."

She wasn't sorry. As much as she admired looking at him in slumber, she enjoyed him awake so much more. "I'm so sorry. I didn't mean to wake you up."

"Honey, that perfume of yours would bring me out of a coma."

"Is it...too strong?"

"Too sexy."

"Oh."

He hadn't bothered to put on any clothes. His boxer shorts were navy-blue and silky-looking. Not that she was actually looking. But when she raised her eyes to meet his, she knew the jig was up. He'd caught her.

Meg was surprised that she didn't feel her face flaming with embarrassment. In fact, she didn't feel embarrassed at all. There wasn't anything wrong with admiring the view. After all, he was giving her a lot of view to work with. And if he wasn't embarrassed, she wouldn't be, either. "Yes," she said in an almost croak.

He tilted his head. "Yes, what?"

"Yes, I like what I'm seeing." Could she be any more brazen?

His smile widened. "Glad to be of service."

She'd like him to service her all right. Unfortunately, she needed to get back to the mansion. As it was, Tina was practically apoplectic.

She waved at the basket. "I brought you some sustenance. Wouldn't want you to waste away to nothing."

"Heaven forbid," he said, then chuckled. "Are you going to join me?"

"I'm sorry, I need to get back."

"I'm sorry, too, but I understand."

"Are you coming back over to haunt us some more?"

"Let me shower and feel halfway human, then I'll be over."

He looked very human to her. Very male and very human. Very male and very sexy and very human. "Okay."

"I'll call your cell phone before I get there in case there's anything I need to know."

"Good idea." Meg turned to go.

"And Meg?"

She swiveled back toward him. "Yes?"

"Thanks for the picnic."

"You're welcome," she said, feeling kind of warm and fuzzy. It was almost a maternal sense of taking care of him. Except she didn't feel the least bit maternal when it came to the man before her. "Be careful with the coffee."

"Why is that?"

"Glenda made it."

"Ah," he said and grinned. "Probably laced, yes?"

"That's a pretty good bet."

"If you aren't careful, all of my inhibitions will be wiped out."

"I'm counting on it," she muttered as she headed toward the door.

MATT RETURNED to the mansion around four o'clock. Meg met him in the east passageway. His hair was still damp from the shower and he smelled of soap and aftershave. He was wearing khaki shorts that revealed a whole lot of muscled leg and a hunter-green T-shirt with the words "Lay It On Me" on it.

Meg wanted to lay it on him all right.

There was something mysteriously wrong with her. Her entire life had been a series of careful decisions. After Mike had jilted her for her sister, she'd vowed to be very, very careful when it came to men. In fact, she'd sworn off men for a long time. But suddenly she had this desire to just let loose. Go with the flow. Use and abuse a man just for pure pleasure.

"You just want to have sex with me, right?" she blurted.

His jaw dropped. "Excuse me?"

Now she finally blushed. Good thing it was pretty dim in the passageway. "I'm certainly picking up vibes. I just want to make sure we're on the same wavelength."

He went still for a moment, but then shrugged. "Name the wave and the length."

"You. Me. Tonight."

"I sort of thought that was a given."

Meg didn't know whether she should be insulted or not. She was brand-new to the fling thing. "That is, if I feel like it," she said.

"You most definitely will."

Her fists plunked down on her hips. "You're awfully sure of yourself."

He smiled again. "Nope, I'm sure of you."

"Meaning what?"

"Meaning you, Ms. Renshaw, go after what you want. And you usually get it."

Now she really was getting irritated. "You think I want you?"

"Yes."

She wanted to smack him just a little less than she wanted to kiss him. "You're pretty full of yourself."

"And you're pretty honest. So am I right?"

"Of course, but you don't have to say so."

"Why not?"

She didn't know. "I don't know."

He cupped her face and kissed her. "Baby, there's no shame in admitting what you want."

"Okay, so I want you."

"Good thing, because I'm dying for you."

She could melt into him right there and then. But they had work to do. Like trying to figure out who killed him. "Well, okay, now that we've come to an understanding—"

He busted out laughing. "An understanding, is it?"

"Right. We're flinging tonight."

His smile would be irritating if it weren't so gorgeous. "I've never heard it turned into a verb before. But it sure works for me."

Meg was too excited to get mad at him. Still, she felt the need to be a step ahead of him. "Okay, well, now that we have our understanding, I need to get to work. Go spook people."

"Yes, ma'am."

MEG NEVER CEASED to amaze Matt. He spent the afternoon following her from room to room and watching as she gently guided the guests through the process of discovering clues. Except she kept making them up as she went along.

The script was completely out the window, yet the guests were having the time of their lives. Even the actors seemed to be having a ball with it all, getting in on the action and pulling off red herrings left and right. By the time everyone was ready to sit down for dinner, Meg had made it fairly impossible for anyone in the place to be in-nocent, including Mr. Danks's cat.

Matt began improvising, too, just for fun. And that was the strange thing. He was really having fun.

As he played spook, the amateur sleuths began talking back to him, asking him questions. He could red herring with the best of them, he decided, pretty proud of himself.

Meg excused herself from the dining room, and Matt knew that meant she was coming back to consult with him. Or tell him off, he didn't know which.

And the truth was, he didn't care which. She'd snuck away several times over the course of the afternoon and each time his blood started pumping overtime and his temperature probably went up several degrees.

She would be his tonight. With any luck, the next several nights. But he'd settle for tonight right now.

She made her way down the passage a few seconds later. Even in her ugly Miss Hatter outfit, she was sexy as hell. And he couldn't wait to be with her.

She stopped in front of him, grinning. "That was kind of rude of you to implicate the cat."

"No, you implicated the cat, I just went with the flow."

"'Follow the cat hair' was inspired."

"I do what I can."

"Mr. Danks is now terrified his cat is going down for the murder."

Matt chuckled. "Who is going down for the murder?"

Meg said, "You'll see."

"Meaning you still don't know."

"Exactly."

"You are something else, sweetheart."

Meg hesitated, then frowned a little. "I'm usually a much better vacation planner than this."

That took him aback. "Are you kidding? With all that's happened, you're doing great."

She gave a rather unladylike snort. "Yeah, right."

"No, really, I mean it." And he did, which totally surprised him. A week ago he'd have fired a woman like Meg on the spot. There'd never, ever been any room for improvisation in his life. And it shocked the hell out of him at how much he'd missed by insisting on a strict schedule of events.

Okay, so he'd become successful. But at what cost? He hadn't had this much fun in... Hmm, when had he had this much fun?

In his entire life he'd taken exactly one vacation. This one. So maybe he was just vacation-deprived, and he would have had as much fun taking a cruise or something.

Somehow he didn't think so.

It was Meg. She made chaos exciting. Which up

until now he would have considered ridiculous. But he had a hard time denying the obvious. This was great, and watching Meg just make things up on the spot was a blast.

"Why don't you just declare a murderer at supper and then we can all go home and…relax?" he suggested.

Even as she tsked, her eyes lit up. "They paid for the weekend, they get the weekend."

"Hey, I paid for the weekend, do I get the weekend?"

"You didn't pay a dime, buddy."

"I haven't sent you my bill for my ghostly performance, yet."

"And I'm still working up the bill for all of Glenda's food and drink you've polished off."

"You drive a hard bargain, Ms. Renshaw."

She studied her nails. "I might be easy, but I'm not cheap, pal."

Matt laughed, kissed her hard, then let her go. "A mere technicality." It was the hardest thing he'd done in a long time, but he stopped himself from dragging her back to the cottage. "Okay, go on back, Ms. Hatter, and do your thing."

"Are you hungry? Thirsty? I'll sneak you something from the kitchen if you'd like."

"No. Lunch was huge. But thank you."

"Well…" She hesitated, which he considered a real plus. "I need to get back to the dinner."

"Go for it."

"I guess…I'll see you later."

Damn straight you will. Probably a lot more of me than you're expecting. "Right. Have fun."

"Right."

MEG RETURNED to the formal dining room, just as Jeeves came in with the salads. She greeted the table of actors with a chill that was so not in her nature, she was amazed that at this stage in her life, she'd learned she could act.

The table holding the guests was abuzz, which she loved. They were taking their sleuthing jobs seriously, but obviously having a good time with it.

"Maybe there's a possibility we haven't thought of," John Hopkins said, around a bite of lettuce. "We haven't even discussed suicide."

"Right. Lots of people do away with themselves by plunging knives into their hearts," replied Ron Warner.

"But see, that's the beauty of it! He was hoping to implicate any or all of the people here."

"It was not suicide," an eerie disembodied voice said, and the chatter died.

Meg had to keep from smiling. Matt was really getting into his role. It was endearing, really. When he wasn't being a stuffed shirt, he sometimes sported a boyish smile that just made mush of her insides.

What his sexy smile did to her some might call indecent. She found it thrilling.

It was so strange. Who invaded Meg's mind and body to bring about such a drastic change in her?

Rhetorical question.

She should be insulted. She wasn't.

Possibly outraged. Nope.

Running scared. Not a chance. Running to the cottage later, maybe.

Meg shook her head. She had work to do, a role to play. She tuned back into the conversation that had begun again after a fairly long silence with fleeting glances from the guests, looking around the room to try to determine the source of the voice.

Little did they know the voice came from the lion's head on the wall. Or, literally, from his roaring mouth.

"What about the maid?" Tammy Warner asked.

"It wasn't her," said Mr. Danks, petting his cat. "I can pretty much vouch for her whereabouts for that entire night."

Meg nearly spit out her iced tea. She stood up. "Ladies and gentlemen, the inspector has informed me he believes he's solved this case."

"I didn't do it," said the actor playing Reed Drew.

"Nor I," chimed in every other actor in the room.

Great. No one did it.

Right then Terence Brogan came staggering into the dining room. Meg hadn't seen him since the first night. In fact, she'd just assumed the man had departed to go nurse his root canal somewhere else. But right now she wanted to kiss his poor, swollen mouth.

"Mr. De Wynter," she said. "Russell, I mean. We're all so sorry for your loss."

"What loss?" the man asked, his eyes bleary.

"Of your brother, of course."

"I don't have—"

"—the time to grieve," Meg said, nodding. "So much to do and so little time." She turned back to the actors. "The detective wants us all to gather tomorrow at brunch, at which time he'll reveal who he suspects killed Lionel De Wynter. We shall see you then."

"The brother!" Lola Hopkins whispered, loud enough to be heard in Florida. "I didn't even think of him."

Neither did I, Meg thought. *Until now.* Poor Mr. Brogan was about to be hauled off to the pokey.

19

HAVING DECIDED who was going to be the ultimate murderer, Meg stuck around just long enough to plant seeds in the guests' minds, then excused herself and ran to Mr. Brogan's room to place fake blood on his makeup case. She'd probably have to buy him a new one, but that was okay.

She also stuck a fake wig inside, which she felt was rather inspired. Then she found Tina and instructed her to type a down and dirty last will and testament for Lionel De Wynter, leaving all of his worldly possessions to his "twin."

"This is a disaster," Tina said.

"Of course it is," Meg said cheerfully. "Leave the will on his bed."

"What are you going to do?"

Meg didn't think she needed to give details. Especially since she didn't know what those details were. She shrugged. "Go to bed."

"With who?"

"Huh?"

"I'm teasing."

"Oh. Well, of course you are."

Except Tina had a shrewd look in her eyes that said she wasn't teasing in the least. For the first time in years, Meg felt like squirming a little. "Well. I'm going…now."

"Where can I find you if I need to?" Tina asked, studying her nails.

"Umm, in my room?"

"Are you asking me or telling me?"

"Just page me," Meg said. "And only if it's an emergency."

"An emergency, right. Say hi to the dead man for me."

Meg's gaze snapped to Tina's. "It's not… I mean it's like… I mean—"

"It's obvious."

"It is?" Meg felt her face flush red-hot. "It's just a fling," she blurted, then wanted to kick herself.

"Of course it is," Tina said. "Now go. Unless the place burns to the ground, you won't be hearing from me."

MATT PACED ACROSS the living room of the cottage, not quite certain why he felt so agitated. It wasn't like this would be his first intimate encounter with a woman. But somehow it felt different.

He felt different.

He couldn't quite place why. Sure, Meg was so unlike any other woman he'd ever met. Well, maybe not unlike some he'd encountered, but unlike any he'd wanted this badly. If he looked back on his track record, he realized he'd always been drawn to successful, driven, focused women.

It wasn't that Meg wasn't successful. In fact, she seemed to be also pretty driven. But focused? Not exactly.

There wasn't anything wrong with Meg's lifestyle, he supposed. In fact, it was rather intriguing. Nothing he could live with for any length of time, but certainly fun for the short term.

But he was uneasy for a reason that didn't make sense. He didn't like to think of the future without her in it in some way. Maybe as friends, occasional lovers, something. Except that didn't jive with his goals.

He was ready for permanent, and she wasn't his idea of permanent.

Except she wasn't his idea of a one-night stand, either.

Confused by all the rambling going on in his head, he didn't even notice she'd arrived until she cleared her throat. He almost jumped through the roof.

Turning, he was happy to note that she'd taken the time to change back into Meg. She wore a peasant dress in muted green and pink, and that stinking wig was long gone. Her rust-brown hair was shiny and free, and her gray eyes looked almost too big for her face.

If he wasn't mistaken, she almost looked scared.

"Hi," he said, for some reason so happy to see her.

"Hi."

"You look good," he commented, because he didn't know what else to say.

"Thank you." She held up a bottle of wine. "Would you like a glass?"

He almost dropped with relief. Something to do to keep from picking her up and dragging her straight to the bedroom.

This was somehow awkward. He knew she'd given him semi-permission to ravish her, but ravishing her instantly didn't feel right. He didn't think he'd ever worried about preliminaries before, unless it involved dinner and a movie or something. "Wine sounds good."

She moved to the kitchenette and he followed her. "How'd the rest of the night go?"

She smiled over her shoulder as she pulled the corkscrew from the drawer. "We have our man."

"We do?"

"Yes, and thanks for the commentary on it not being suicide."

"What commentary?"

"When you responded that it wasn't suicide."

"When did I do that?"

She stopped in mid-cork-pull. "At dinner tonight."

He shook his head. "I left as soon as you did."

The wine bottle hit the counter with a thunk. "Are you telling me you didn't say, 'It wasn't suicide' into the mike?"

"Sorry, wasn't me."

"Oh, boy."

"Are you sure it wasn't just someone in the dining room?"

"Positive."

"Oh, boy."

"Our ghost?"

"There's no such thing—"

"—as ghosts. Yes, I know. But someone or something was talking to the group. If it wasn't you…"

It definitely wasn't him, but he didn't want her spooked, either. There had to be a perfectly logical explanation. He just couldn't come up with one at the moment. "Maybe I did, and just forgot. Lack of sleep and all."

Her eyes narrowed with worry. "Would you like to get some sleep?"

"No! I mean, no, I'm not tired any longer." He searched for something to distract her. "So who's the guilty party?"

"Your twin brother."

"Huh?"

"You remember the guy that was supposed to play you in the first place?"

"Oh, right. The drunk guy."

"Technically, no. But it works for our purposes." She pulled two goblets from the upper cabinet and poured the red wine. "Well, he showed up at supper unexpectedly. In fact, I thought he'd left the estate. So he's your murderer."

Matt grinned. "That was kind of rude of him."

"Well, he inherits your wealth, and all."

"Ungrateful brat."

Meg laughed, handing him his wine. "The funny thing is, he doesn't even know it yet."

Matt clinked her glass, then took a sip of the cabernet. Finally he took a deep breath. "I don't really want wine."

She went still. "What do you want?"

"You."

Her goblet landed hard. "Oh."

"What do you want?"

"I'm not quite sure."

Matt took a step closer to her. "What does that mean?"

"I barely know you, for one."

He nodded. "I can't argue with that."

"Try."

He sipped at his wine while he tried to find a convincing argument. "You can't deny you're attracted to me." He stopped. "Can you?"

Her head shook. "No, I can't deny it."

"Good, then we agree on that much."

"Okay."

"What else?"

"There's no future in this."

That stopped him in mid-sip. "Did you want there to be a future in this?"

"No!" she said a little too adamantly for his taste. "I mean," she added, "we have such different goals."

Matt nodded. "That's true. But if we both understand that going in, then we're not fooling ourselves or each other."

"Really?"

Matt set down his wine. "Really. But the plain truth is, I thought you were beautiful and sexy from the moment I saw you sprawled on the ground."

Her laughter was just a little shaky. "I thought you were pretty cute, too."

"And you can't deny that this would have happened last night if we weren't...interrupted."

"True again."

"So why the qualms now?"

"Something just feels different."

"What?" he asked, although he felt the same way. Something was different. He just couldn't put his finger on it.

"I don't know. It's like the stakes have gone up, but I don't know why."

Exactly. "Well, if it doesn't feel right, I'm not going to push it."

"That's kind of rude of you."

His heart tripped a little. "It is?"

"This is no time to be a gentleman, Mr. Rossi."

"It's not?"

"No, it's not."

He paused for a second, set down his goblet and grinned. "Well, all righty then." He grabbed her shoulders and pulled her against him, inhaling the slightly flowery scent of her perfume. "In that case, Ms. Renshaw, prepare to be seduced."

"Much better," she murmured, right before his lips covered hers.

SOMEHOW THEIR CLOTHES laid a path from the kitchen to the bedroom, so that by the time they hit the bed, they were both naked.

Meg would have laughed at the way Matt hip-hopped out of his jeans and boxers if she weren't so busy ogling his torso. He was gorgeous. There wasn't a doubt in her mind that he was an accomplished athlete. You didn't get those abs and those pecs by channel-surfing.

Meg had never been particularly self-conscious about her body. The two men she'd been naked with had seemed to appreciate her figure. So she wasn't too afraid he'd find her disgusting. What was killing her was the uncertainty of just how well she could bring this man pleasure.

He was arguably the most handsome man she'd ever met. So to continue the argument, he'd probably had his share of women. Meg was a little intimidated at where she'd stack up among his conquests.

Did she like being considered a conquest? She didn't know, but the way he kissed her left her little room to dwell on the notion.

She'd never experienced this sense of ravishment before. It was like he owned her mouth, and he was going to plunder it at will.

And his hands seemed to be everywhere. Just when she thought she'd faint from the feel of his palm on her breast, his hand would slide down her skin to cup her bottom. And just when she realized how good that felt, he leaned down to suckle on her neck.

"Meg, you feel so good," he whispered against her suddenly hot flesh.

"Oh, so do you," she murmured, and no truer words had ever passed her lips.

His body was rock hard in all the right places. She couldn't get enough of pressing her skin to his. He smelled like soap and something else elusive. But very, very sexy.

Matt picked her up and gently laid her on the bed, then fell on top of her without ever taking his lips from her throat.

One of them moaned, but she wasn't sure if it was her or Matt, or maybe both. All she knew was she couldn't get enough of his hands. Or his lips.

Meg's senses were reeling. She felt so needy. And by the feverish way his hands traveled over her, she knew it wasn't just her.

"Show me where you want me touching you," Matt rasped.

And she did, directing his hand between her legs. And oh, how he touched her. Meg nearly screamed at the sensation of his fingers exploring her, invading her more than willing body.

His mouth came down on her breast, and she arched up with a cry. Between his lips and his hands, he was driving her insane in the best possible way.

Meg's hand slipped down his body, and she wrapped her palm around him. Apparently he liked that, if his groan of pain and pleasure was any measure.

An orgasm crashed through her and she cried out. Matt lifted his head and smiled at her, a sleepy, satisfied look on his face.

"Inside me. Now," she croaked. "Now."

He spread her legs apart even more and pushed into her, and Meg thought she was going to die of happiness at the sensation of this big man filling her, thrusting with a fervor that made her blood sing.

Within seconds she was riding the wave all

over again, and before she knew it, it crashed over her, through her, in her. She stopped thinking and just felt.

And oh, she felt him come in her, heard his hiss of pleasure. It was the most beautiful moment in her life. And as he slowed his hips and looked at her, she knew that he'd experienced the same thing.

It was special. It was right. They were right.

His upper body held a slight sheen and she didn't know if it came from him or her, because right now her flesh felt on fire.

"Thank you," she whispered, then felt a little foolish. Did one thank a man for good sex? She never had before, so she wasn't sure.

"Thank you," he whispered back.

"Catch your breath. We're doing that again real soon."

He slid out of her with a chuckle, laid on his side and draped his arm over her belly. "Are you trying to kill me, woman?"

"How can I? You're already dead."

"Oh, yeah. In that case, brace yourself."

Meg had so many words on her lips, but she bit them back. She had to remember that this was temporary. Even if it was the most wonderful thing she ever remembered in her life, it was not for keeps. And she wasn't going to make a fool of herself by uttering endearments.

"What just happened here?" Matt said, brushing her hair from her forehead.

She was afraid to answer, so she just kissed his collarbone. "What do you mean?"

"I...guess I'm just blown away," he said, after a pause.

"Oh, me, too!"

"Yeah?"

"Yeah. I...this was kind of amazing."

He kept silent for a moment, then said quietly, "Where do we go from here, Meg?"

"I don't know."

"I'm not sure I can forget this. Us."

She swallowed a small sob. "I'll never forget you. Or this."

"But it doesn't change anything, does it?"

She didn't know. All she knew was she planned on a lot more Matt for the next few days. Thinking beyond that was depressing.

"Meg?"

"Hmm?"

"I, umm, forgot protection. I didn't mean to, I swear. I just wasn't thinking."

He looked so boyishly contrite that she chuckled. "I'm on the pill, Matt. You have nothing to worry about."

"Oh."

She could swear he almost looked disappointed. And it occurred to her that he might have forgotten on purpose. But no, she didn't believe that. Matt wasn't the type to trap a woman like that. She didn't know a lot of things about him at this point, but she'd stake her life on that one. Matt had more honor than that. And besides, he planned his life down to the millisecond. He wouldn't purposely leave something that monumental to chance. Not to mention, he didn't love her. Why would he try to get a woman he didn't love pregnant?

Another depressing thought. He didn't love her.

Not that she loved him. Unfortunately, she wasn't so sure right now. Something very special just happened being with him this way. And the thought of it all coming to a crashing end held no appeal at all.

She'd think about it more thoroughly as the weekend drew to a close. Right now she just wanted to enjoy what they had at this moment.

"Matt?"

"Yes?"

"I want you again."

"Trust me, love, I want you, too."

Her fingers fluttered down his body. "So, like you said, brace yourself, cowboy."

"Oh, Lord, Meg. You are going to be the death of me." His fingers found her again. "But what a way to go."

20

BY THE TIME everyone gathered in the dining room for brunch the next morning, Meg ached more than she ever remembered in her life.

Strangely enough, for as little as she'd slept last night, she wasn't in the least bit tired. In fact, she felt exhilarated. When she'd left Matt this morning he'd been deep in sleep, and she hadn't had the heart to wake him, considering how much she'd pestered him throughout the night.

He'd been a good sport about it, though, she thought with a grin.

Of course, when she'd walked into the study this morning, Tina had given her a thorough once-over, then said, "That good, huh?"

She at first resisted the urge to shout "Yes!" thinking it was a private matter between her and Matt, but apparently the smile on her face said it all because Tina just shook her head and said, "I smell disaster."

Problem was, Meg had the feeling Tina was

right on with that assessment. Because sometime during the night she'd fallen hard for Matthew Rossi, entrepreneur.

But she wasn't ready to give the man what he wanted, and even if she were, she wasn't sure that he even considered her good lifelong material.

He'd acted as though he worshiped her, but that was probably pure lust. They were so different. Their goals were incompatible. At least for now.

And Meg couldn't imagine asking Matt to put his goals on hold while she finished growing up. He just wasn't an "on hold" type of guy. It was too unfair to ask him to wait for her biological clock to kick in.

What if it never did? What if she hit thirty, or thirty-five, and still had no desire to have children? If she cared about him at all, which she realized she did—very much—there was no way she could ask him to set his desires aside just for her.

But it was going to kill her to walk away.

Meg shook off the depressing thought. She had a murder to solve, and all the players were in place, except for the murderer himself, who Jeeves would escort into the room at the appropriate time. If Jeeves could get the man to stand straight.

The actor playing Detective Tracy arrived, just as everyone sat down for the meal. "Ladies and gentlemen," he intoned, "I am utterly stumped. Unless you've unearthed more clues than I have, I'm afraid that the murder of Mr. Lionel De Wynter might never be solved." He turned to the guests. "At this point, good people, it's time for you to join in the debate."

That's when Meg remembered that she'd forgotten to inform the actor of the change in plans. At this point, it didn't matter. They could name Fluffy the cat as the murderer and she'd agree to it. Before she held another mystery weekend, she'd have to work on her technique.

Mr. Holmes stood up and pointed at Meg. "There's your murderer, Detective."

"But she was with us when Mr. De Wynter was killed," Mr. Danks argued.

Lola Hopkins chimed in, "But we found the tape recorder, remember? She could have murdered him earlier and then played the tape to give herself an alibi."

Oops, Meg had forgotten about that. She pretty much sucked at this murder mystery business.

"I know nothing about any tape recorder," she said.

"So you say," said Mr. Drew.

"We checked the tape player and found no prints on it," improvised Detective Tracy.

"I say it was Agatha Bond," said Tammy Warner. "There was a feather in the master bedroom, and she's the only one who wears boas."

Agatha stood indignantly. "Yes, I went to see Lionel, but only to plead with him not to take the course of action he'd chosen. When I left he was very much alive, and still a jerk. I'm not crying in my soup that he's dead, but I certainly didn't kill him."

"The ghost told us to follow the cat hair. That leads me to believe it was the maid."

"I told you," Mr. Danks said, "she was with me."

Meg was getting a headache. It was time to steer them on the right track. "Who had the most to gain by Mr. De Wynter's demise? Certainly not me. I'm out of a job."

"He jilted you."

Meg waved that notion away. "Men like him are a dime a dozen." Meg heard a faintly concealed sputter behind the wall. "But health insurance benefits don't grow on trees." She sighed. "I repeat, who had the most to gain?"

"They all did. He was going to ruin the lot of them."

Just then Jeeves came into the room. "Miss Hatter, may I have a word?"

They stepped out into the foyer. "Yes?"

"Mr. Brogan. He's gone."

"Excuse me?"

"Mr. Brogan. Gone."

"Our murderer bailed on us?"

"Indeed."

Meg chewed her lip. "How'd you like to be a murderer?"

"Not particularly."

"I thought not. Well, thanks for telling me."

"Disaster," Tina said, coming up behind her.

"Yes, it is."

Meg walked back into the dining room, trying to think. Her eyes lit on the inspector. Why not? "I've just been informed that Mr. De Wynter's brother has left rather abruptly."

"So he *did* do it!" said Ron Warner. "See, Tammy, I *told* you it was the brother."

"If it was, he had an accomplice," Meg said. She tried to think what she could possibly say to back up that claim. "Because at the time of Lionel's murder, his brother Russell was out cold." She turned to the detective. "I ask again, who had the most to gain by Mr. De Wynter's death?"

All eyes landed on the faux cop. He looked around and swallowed. Either he was actually nervous, or he was going with the flow.

"Wait a minute," said John Hopkins. "Now that I think about it, the detective here showed up only moments after we discovered the body."

"Yeah, how'd he get here so soon?"

"But what did he have to gain?"

Good question. "Has anyone taken a close look at the will?"

"What will?"

"The one in Mr. De Wynter's brother's room?"

"We couldn't get into his room," Lola said. "It was locked."

"Then you didn't know that Detective Tracy's sister is married to Russell De Wynter?" Meg said, flying by the seat of her pants at an alarming rate.

"That was in the will?"

"Yes, it was," Meg said. "I drew it up myself. In the case of Mr. De Wynter's death, all of his assets, other than a few bequests, go to his brother Russell. In the event of Russell's demise, Detective Tracy's sister inherits."

"Ohhhhhhh," the entire room, including the actors, said in unison. Meg just barely heard the sound of a low, masculine chuckle coming from the lion's mouth.

"My guess is," Meg added, warming to the new ending, "that the next time we see Russell De Wynter, he won't be breathing either."

"This is ridiculous," said Detective Tracy, adjusting his tie nervously. "I had no idea what was in Mr. De Wynter's will."

"Sure," said Mr. Danks, stroking his kitty excitedly. "The detective came here, murdered Mr. De Wynter, then made certain he was the first on the scene so he could plant clues that made everyone else look guilty. The old bait and switch."

Meg didn't know what a bait and switch was, but she could live with that.

"Then sometime last night or today, he came back and murdered Mr. De Wynter's brother so his sister would inherit all the money."

"You can't prove any of this," said the detective, who Meg wanted to kiss for going with the bait and switch flow.

"Ma'am?" said Molly the Maid from the doorway.

"Yes, Molly?" Meg said.

"I think I've found Mr. De Wynter."

"Which one?" Meg asked, worried Molly had stumbled across Matt.

"The brother, ma'am."

"Where is he?"

"In the rose garden."

"Is he…alive?"

"Doesn't look like it, ma'am."

A collective gasp went up from the crowd. Meg rushed out the door, to the kitchen and out the French doors to the back garden. She heard banging feet behind her, but was too worried Terence Brogan had actually kicked it to pay much attention.

Sure enough, he was facedown on the ground. Meg felt for a pulse, and almost sobbed with relief when she felt the faint beating in his wrist.

She dropped his arm and turned around. "Dead all right," she said. "Everyone inside," she added, before the man could groan or wake up. "Where is the detective?"

Nowhere to be found, is where the detective was. Meg put in a fake call to the police to report him, then gathered everyone in the dining room again. "Okay, well, by my calculations, Mr. Danks solved the case. He wins the magician's weekend for two in the Adirondacks."

Molly the Maid sneezed and said, "Oh, I love magic!"

Meg kept herself from rolling her eyes. "So, are y'all ready for brunch?"

"THAT WAS A DISASTER," Tina said.

Meg threw off her wig. "Yes, it was."

"But it was fun," Tina said, almost making Meg keel over.

"The guests had fun, I think."

"They did. They were bubbling all over the place."

"Then we won."

"Where are you going?" Tina asked, as she followed hot on Meg's heels.

"To go unearth a dead guy."

"Disaster," Tina said.

"Don't I know it?"

MEG AND MATT sat on the couch in the cottage. Meg seemed deep in thought, and Matt didn't want to interrupt whatever was going on in her head. But finally he couldn't stand it. "That was brilliant."

She laughed. "That was ridiculous."

"In a brilliantly ridiculous way."

"You're just being a flatterer, Mr. Rossi. I'll be lucky to have a job by the end of the week."

"You could come work for me," he said, then stopped, not having a clue where that thought had come from.

She stared at him. "You've got to be kidding me."

"Not at all."

"What would I do for you?"

He thought about that. "Manage some of my properties?"

She shook her head. "It wouldn't work."

"Why not?"

"I don't want you as my boss, Matt."

"Hey, I'm a good boss!"

"I'm sure you are. That's not the point."

"What's the point, Meg?"

"I don't know. I just know that isn't it."

He took a deep breath. "So this is it?"

Her eyes teared up, which just about broke his heart. "I guess it is."

"Why?"

She swiped at her cheeks. "You know why. What you want and what I want are not the same things."

"What we had last night seemed to be pretty damn compatible, Meg."

Her laughter sounded just slightly hysterical. "That was sex. You can get that anywhere."

"I don't want it anywhere. I want it with you."

Her sigh was part hiccup. "I'm not ready for children, Matt. I'm just not. And I know you are."

"That's true, I am. But I can wait for a while."

"What if I never change my mind?"

He stared at her. She was such a sweet, nurturing soul, he couldn't imagine it. He understood the root, but he still didn't understand that she might never want to have children. Didn't all women want children?

"Not all women want children," she said quietly.

Matt's mind mentally ticked off his list. Could he live with not ever having children?

"You couldn't live with never having children," she said, and he started to wonder if she was a mind reader. "And I couldn't ask you to give up that dream. You'd grow to resent me."

"So this is it," he said, and couldn't believe how deeply it hurt. It wasn't until he woke up this morning to find her gone that he'd realized how empty that cottage, that bed, his heart were without her.

"Well, I'd say keep in touch," she said, but her voice was most definitely bordering on breaking. "But I'm not sure that would be good for either of us."

"You mean, not see each other at all?"

She faced him and took his hands. "Don't you see, I can't do that to you."

"Oh, yes, seeing you would be such a hardship. How dare you try to subject me to such a thing."

She squeezed. "Look, if I kept you from your goals, it would kill me. Every time I'd see you looking at a kid, I'd feel horrible. Every time I'd see a woman who is so ready for a special man like you in her life, I'd feel I was cheating you. It won't work."

"So you're willing to throw us away."

Her eyebrows rose. "I didn't know there *was* an us."

"Well, there won't be if we just walk away from each other now."

"I need time to think, Matt. And while I'm doing that thinking, I don't want to bind you or limit you or keep you from reaching for your dream. It's just not fair. And I…care about you too much to let that happen. And I care about me enough that I don't want to have that hanging over my head."

Any other man might take her at her word. Matt wasn't about to do that. This was too important. He and Meg might be oil and vinegar, but those ingredients made for a delicious salad. But pushing her now would be a mistake. A big one. He knew enough about negotiation to know when to give his opponent breathing space.

"Okay, Meg," he said quietly. "Go back to your job and your life. I'm not going to try to force you into making a decision you aren't ready to make."

He cupped her face. "But remember this. The last few days have been the most fun I've had in my life. It wasn't the dumb murder game, it was you. And it wasn't just the sex. It was the thrill of not knowing what you'd do next."

"You'd get tired of that soon enough."

"You don't know that."

Meg jumped up, pacing. "I just want what's right for both of us."

"I know. I appreciate that. But when you get the chance, remind me to tell you what I think is best for me. And you."

Meg smiled weakly. "I will. I promise."

Matt stood as well. His next words were the hardest he'd ever have to force past his lips. "I'm going to head out today. Just know that you can call me anytime."

"Thank you."

He stuck his hands in the front pockets of his jeans. "I've loved meeting you."

Her forehead wrinkled with distress. "Right back atcha."

"I've loved…spending time with you."

"Ditto," she squeaked.

He was about to open his mouth to try to utter the three words that might convince her not to do this, but his fingers closed over a piece of paper in his pocket he didn't remember putting there. He pulled it out and unfolded it.

His mouth must have dropped open, because Meg said, "What is it?" with alarm in her voice.

He couldn't find his voice, so he just handed the strangely scrawled note over to her.

She read aloud, "You make a lousy ghost. Leave it to the pros."

"THIS IS A DISASTER," Tina said, exactly one month after the murder mystery weekend.

Considering they were sitting in the Atlanta office, finalizing the details of a cruise vacation package with a stand-up comic theme, Meg didn't quite know what the disaster was. "What is?"

"You."

"What about me?"

"You are miserable."

Meg sat back and tossed down her pen. "Is that right?"

"Damn straight."

"What gave me away?" Meg asked, although she could hardly deny it. She *was* miserable.

"You never smile, you never laugh, you stare out the window as if waiting for something. In other words, you just aren't any fun anymore."

Meg couldn't remember ever seeing a hint of fun in Tina's demeanor, so she was a little befuddled. "I'm sorry if you're finding me so boring."

Tina shook her head. "It's not boring. It's painful."

That pinched at Meg's heart. She certainly didn't want to cause anyone else pain, although she felt like she had enough to go around for everyone in Atlanta.

It wasn't that she hadn't talked to Matt in the last month, she had. He called at least once a week to ask how she was. She'd never lied so much in her life as she tried to cheerfully make him think all was right with the world.

All was not all right with the world. The void was tearing her apart. But even after a month, she hadn't figured out a happy solution to their dilemma.

They wanted different things and the same things at one and the same time.

"I'm sorry, Tina. I really am."

"Well, do something about it, then."

"I don't know what to do about it."

"Well, off the top of my head, I'd say how about calling him?"

"And saying what?"

"'I love you,' for instance?"

"I can't."

"Three words. Easy."

"In principle, not so much."

"You do, don't you?"

Meg dropped her head in her hands. "Yes, I do."

"Then say it, dammit. Put us all out of our misery."

With that, Tina marched out of her office, with self-righteous indignation.

Meg pondered it for she didn't know how long. She didn't know what would happen if she took that step, but anything was better than bottling up this awful feeling of loss. And obviously she wasn't bottling well, if Tina, and probably every friend she had, had noticed.

After a while, she pulled her phone book from her desk and looked up his cell phone number. Dialing, she both hoped and dreaded him answering.

At the moment she was certain she'd get his voice mail, he picked up, sounding rather grumpy. "Rossi."

She hesitated, and he said, "Hello?"

"I love you," she blurted, then disconnected.

She didn't know what she expected. Him calling her back instantly? Or ignoring the message, because it could be from any number of his female acquaintances? Or worse, ignoring it because he knew precisely who had uttered those words?

A miserable hour later she concluded that he hadn't wanted to hear those words from her, seeing as he hadn't attempted to call her back.

Well, there was her answer.

Meg rose wearily from her desk, realizing she'd been a useless lump all day. Even Tina was avoiding her. She wasn't doing anyone any favors hanging around the office.

She wanted to kick herself for being so stupid as to take Tina's advice. If Tina didn't predict disasters, she had a future in creating them.

Waving perfunctorily at the office staff, she headed toward the front doors, staring at the ground. She nearly ran into a delivery boy, carrying flowers. She tried to smile, but didn't quite pull it off.

She was almost through the door when Mary, the receptionist, stopped her. "Meg! These are for you."

Meg stopped dead and turned around. "Are you sure?"

Mary tsked. "Well, let's see, last I checked we only had five or so Megan Renshaws working for us."

Meg's heart leapt, and she nearly sprinted back to the reception desk. The flowers weren't the standard roses, but a huge bouquet of just about everything in the book.

She dropped her briefcase and, with shaking hands, pulled the card from the envelope with her name on it.

"I love you, too. My plane gets into Hartsford from Chicago at 7:30 p.m. Please meet me there."

MEG WASN'T JUST ON TIME for Matt's arrival, she was actually an hour and a half early.

She found his terminal, then headed for the lounge to nurse a glass of sherry and go over and over in her head what she wanted to say to him.

In the end, she couldn't say anything, because the sight of him was so breath-stealing, she couldn't get her vocal cords to cooperate.

He kissed her, right there in front of a crowd of hundreds, if not thousands.

They didn't say a word to one another until they were seated in a rented limo, heading for who knew where. He hadn't even checked luggage.

When they were on their way, he raised the privacy glass between them and the driver, then turned to her.

"Matt—"

"Meg—"

They both stopped, then laughed. Meg waited this time.

"You look beautiful, Meg."

"You, too," she said, with all the brilliance of a moron.

"I've missed you like crazy."

"I've missed you, too."

"What took you so long?" he asked.

"I…well…I had to wallow in misery for a while so I could figure out what an idiot I am."

"No, honey," he said softly, brushing her cheek with his knuckles. "You are no idiot."

"Oh, yes, I am."

"Being honest enough to walk away when you thought I cared more about a stupid list of goals than you is *not* being an idiot." He sucked in a breath. "Being honest and brave enough to make that call today is *not* being an idiot."

"Matt," she said, "I don't know how we're going to work this out. I just know I've been so unhappy."

"I'll tell you how we work this out," Matt said. "We take each day as it comes, but instead of apart, we take them together."

Oh, that worked for her. Meg didn't know how this was all going to end, but she knew she couldn't let Matthew Rossi go without giving them a shot.

"What if I…what if I said I don't know when I'll be ready?"

"We'll know when we know, Meg. That's good enough for me. It sure as hell beats the alternative, which is no solution whatsoever."

"I'm not quitting my job."

"Heaven forbid. There are too many murder mystery weekends to screw up in your future."

"When will we ever get to see each other?"

"Funny you should mention that. I opened an Atlanta office less than a week after leaving Charleston."

"Really?"

"I wanted to be close by in case you came to your senses."

"Oh, Matt. What are we going to do with each other?"

"Love each other."

"I'm going to drive you crazy."

"I know, isn't it great?"

She laughed, even while tears streamed unheeded down her face. "We'll see how you feel about that in the future."

"Nothing could be worse than not having you, Ms. Renshaw."

"I love you, Matt."

"I know, isn't it great?"

"This would be a good time to tell me you love me, too."

"Right now?"

"The sooner the better."

He smiled, and her heart melted to mush. "I love you, Meg. More than I ever thought possible, for an irritating, make it up as you go along, flighty—"

She grabbed the lapels of his suit coat. "Should have quit while you were ahead."

"Just couldn't wait to see what you'd do next."

And she showed him.

ATHENA FORCE

The Athena Academy adventure continues....

Three secret sisters
Three super talents
One unthinkable legacy...

The ties that bind may be the ties that kill as these extraordinary women race against time to beat the genetic time bomb that is their birthright....

Don't miss the latest three stories in the Athena Force continuity

DECEIVED by Carla Cassidy, January 2005

CONTACT by Evelyn Vaughn, February 2005

PAYBACK by Harper Allen, March 2005

And coming in April–June 2005, the final showdown for Athena Academy's best and brightest!

Available at your favorite retail outlet.

If you enjoyed what you just read,
then we've got an offer you can't resist!

Take 2 bestselling love stories FREE!

Plus get a FREE surprise gift!

Clip this page and mail it to Harlequin Reader Service®

IN U.S.A.	IN CANADA
3010 Walden Ave.	P.O. Box 609
P.O. Box 1867	Fort Erie, Ontario
Buffalo, N.Y. 14240-1867	L2A 5X3

YES! Please send me 2 free Harlequin Flipside™ novels and my free surprise gift. After receiving them, if I don't wish to receive anymore, I can return the shipping statement marked cancel. If I don't cancel, I will receive 2 brand-new novels every month, before they're available in stores! In the U.S.A., bill me at the bargain price of $4.24 plus 50¢ shipping & handling per book and applicable sales tax, if any*. In Canada, bill me at the bargain price of $4.94 plus 50¢ shipping & handling per book and applicable taxes**. That's the complete price—what a great deal! I understand that accepting the 2 free books and gift places me under no obligation ever to buy any books. I can always return a shipment and cancel at any time. Even if I never buy another book from Harlequin, the 2 free books and gift are mine to keep forever.

131 HDN DZ9H
331 HDN DZ9J

Name	(PLEASE PRINT)

Address		Apt.#

City	State/Prov.	Zip/Postal Code

Not valid to current Harlequin Flipside™ subscribers.

Want to try two free books from another series?
Call 1-800-873-8635 or visit www.morefreebooks.com.

* Terms and prices subject to change without notice. Sales tax applicable in N.Y.
** Canadian residents will be charged applicable provincial taxes and GST.
All orders subject to approval. Offer limited to one per household.
® and ™ are registered trademarks owned and used by the trademark owner and or its licensee.

© 2004 Harlequin Enterprises Ltd.   FLIPS04R

Curl up and have a

Heart *to* Heart

with

Harlequin Romance®

Just like having a heart-to-heart
with your best friend, these stories
will take you from laughter to tears
and back again. So heartwarming
and emotional you'll want to
have some tissues handy!

Next month Harlequin is thrilled to bring you
Natasha Oakley's first book for Harlequin Romance:

For Our Children's Sake (#3838),
on sale March 2005

Then watch out for....

A Family For Keeps (#3843),
by Lucy Gordon, on sale May 2005

Available wherever Harlequin books are sold.

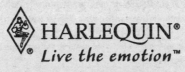

HARLEQUIN®
Live the emotion™

www.eHarlequin.com   HRHTH